BEYOND THE GRID

Beyond The Grid Book 1

CONNOR MCCOY

CHAPTER ONE

JACOB ABRUPTLY PUT the brakes on, slowing the car just as it hit the dirt road coming off Virginia's State Road 219. He gently chided himself for slowing down this far from the place that he soon would call home. He was being too eager. He wanted to disembark as soon as possible, but that just would leave him and his wife with a longer trail to walk to the homestead's front door. However, he could not help himself. He had been waiting for this day for years. Now he was here!

Jacob turned to the young lady in the passenger seat. "You want me to pull up?"

The woman shook her head, swishing her long hair around. "No." She unlocked her door. "Actually, I wouldn't mind running to the front door!"

Jacob chuckled. "A race, huh?"

After opening his door, he rose from the car seat but banged his head against the roof. "Shit!" he whispered. This car was too low to the ground. At almost six feet tall, Jacob Avery was an ill fit for this four-door car. Oh well. He had been planning to get rid of the car anyway, as it would not be a proper fit for their new life.

Once he stood up and quickly shook his legs, he dashed after his wife, although with her head start, Jacob was unlikely to catch up to her. Domino's thin but fit frame made her a quick and nimble gal. Jacob could not recall catching up to her unless she wanted him to do so.

However, this time he finished just a few steps behind her in the shadow of the homestead's porch, to his own surprise. Domino was leaning against the wooden support post, catching her breath. Usually, she could run for a longer distance without petering out. Was she alright?

"Guess that was a hell of a run after all," Jacob said.

Domino wiped a slick of sweat from her forehead. "Guess so, huh?" She rubbed her stomach as she took a look at the home siding. "Damn, this place needs a little work, don't you think?"

A little work? The homestead before them certainly could use more than that. From a distance, the house looked fine, even charming, with the wrap-around porch and sloping roof, topped by a second floor with its own sloped roof. But upon closer inspection, the wooden panels were in a clear state of disrepair, and the white paint was faded, frayed. The porch gutter also hung loose from its moorings.

"That's what makes it perfect." Jacob peeled off a loose sliver of siding. "We can remake this place into what we want. It's going to be ours from bottom to top."

"And, of course, it came with a cheap price tag," Domino said with a grin.

"It had to." Jacob peeled off another loose piece of siding. "If we wanted to start our new life out here, we had to take what we can get." He pivoted off his right heel, turning himself toward the view of the Blue Ridge Mountains beyond the porch.

Domino left the post, her wooden heels making soft clomps on the porch's surface as she approached her husband. She knew what he was thinking. "It's beautiful," she said with a sigh, "No more graffiti. No brick walls." She waved her hand in front of her face. "No car exhaust." She fished her hands around Jacob's right arm, covering the ink tattoo that ran across his forearm. "No noise," she said with a soothing whisper.

That last part especially appealed to Jacob. There was no one around for miles. They were a few yards off the nearest road. This property was bathed in blissful silence. It bore no resemblance to their old life in the busy suburbs of Washington D.C. Who cared if the house looked as if it had taken a beating?

His wife released her grip, uncovering his tattoo. Jacob had given up a lot to buy this house. He recently had had laser surgery to remove a tattoo that ran down the left side of his face. He could have taken off the tattoos on his arms as well, but he was not willing to spend another year up in the D.C. suburbs. It was time to leave.

The money Jacob would have used to remove his other tattoos instead went toward buying this farmland. He could live with the tattoos for longer, for years if necessary. With the expenses to come, from renovating the house to building the wooden fences that would surround his crop rows, Jacob could not imagine he would have money to remove the rest of his tattoos anytime soon.

Domino patted her stomach. “Jacob, I think our dream might be coming true sooner than you think.”

Jacob gazed at Domino. His eyes widened. Was she really hinting at what he was thinking of?

Domino grinned. “I have been feeling very hungry lately. Think I’m eating for two now?”

Jacob couldn’t believe it. He had been so focused on purchasing this homestead he didn’t figure his family was about to grow. *Thank God I didn’t wait another year to buy a place out here*, he thought.

“What do you think our first is going to be like?” Domino asked.

JUBILEE’S FIST slammed into the punching bag. Brandon held onto the bag with all of his strength.

The bag was suspended from the ceiling by a chain, but Jubilee's blow easily would have sent it flying into the back wall without someone to hold it. Brandon was intrigued. A nine-year-old boy bracing a punching bag against the strength of an athletic fifteen-year-old girl? He was curious to learn which of them would give out first.

The force of Jubilee's blow slid Brandon back a few steps. That was a good hit, but not unexpected. Brandon knew his sister's blows well. He had witnessed many of them over the past few years. Thankfully, he never was on the wrong end of any of them. He wouldn't want to, even if he wore protective training gear.

Then she struck again. This time Brandon popped off the bag and fell to the soft carpeted floor.

Okay, he didn't expect *that* big of a blow. Jubilee was in hard charging form this morning.

Brandon bounced back up. Jubilee was so into her routine she struck the bag again without Brandon holding onto it. The bag nearly flew right into Brandon's face. Reacting quickly, Brandon rolled across the floor to avoid the swinging bag.

"Hit the pause button!" Brandon cried as he dashed back to the bag. Jubilee stopped.

After steadying the bag, he said, "Okay, go!"

Jubilee hit it a few more times before she stopped to catch her breath. Brandon was so relieved that his grip slipped. He dropped down flat onto the floor, but without hurting himself. He had learned from training with Jubilee how to take falls.

"Okay, I'm ready," Jubilee said.

Brandon looked up at his sister's tall stature. Brandon was sweating hard through his orange shirt and baggy shorts, but Jubilee only trickled a few drops down her muscled arms and legs. Her athletic clothing barely looked wrinkled, even from all the blows she just had thrown.

"Are you even human?" Brandon asked.

Jubilee rolled her eyes. "We've just started. You know how long I can go on the first round."

"Yeah." Brandon picked himself up. "Forever." He straightened out his bunched-up shirt. "Mister Valance had to pick today not to come."

Ordinarily, Jubilee's trainer, Mister Mike Valance, would be here to shepherd her through her mixed martial arts training, but every now and then he had to take a rain check. When he did, Brandon would step in to help out Jubilee.

"Mister Valance's daughter is turning thirteen today," Jubilee replied.

Brandon's cheeks burned. He didn't know that. "Fine." As he stretched out his arms, he thought of how to delay Jubilee from resuming punching. "Uh, have you come up with a name?" Brandon asked.

"A name? A name for what?" Jubilee asked.

"You know, your MMA fighting name," Brandon replied, "How about, 'The Jubilation?'" He spread out his arms over his head. "What do you think? I like it!"

With a smirk, Jubilee raised her fists. “I think I’m fine with my own name.”

Resigned to his fate, Brandon held on to the punching bag once more. This small room was built off the edge of the house, accessible through the home’s den, one of their father’s add-ons since he and Mom had moved in here. Their mother insisted that the punching bag not be in Jubilee’s bedroom because the teen would be too tempted to practice on it even through the night or when she should be doing her homework. Brandon could not be happier that his mom insisted on that. His room was next door to hers and he didn’t want to be serenaded with the sounds of pounding and shouting as he tried finishing his homework or working on one his building projects. He was fond of making models or devices with pulleys and tackles. His mom said he had a wonderfully creative mind.

But with today being Saturday, they were off from homeschooling. Instead of their mother giving them their lessons, they were free to indulge in whatever leisure activities they wished, provided their chores were completed.

Pow! Brandon went sprawling to the floor.

Activities that included Jubilee’s training.

A little dazed, Brandon stood back up and grabbed onto the bag. But Jubilee, mercifully, did not throw another punch. She stopped to catch her breath again.

“Hey,” Brandon said, “we should...” He quit

talking for a moment to catch a deep breath. He wanted to think of something else that would catch his sister's interest. "We should go to...to the pond! The bluegills, they..."

"Right. They're spawning now, aren't they?" Jubilee asked.

Brandon nodded. "Want to grab some cane poles?"

Jubilee pulled off her gloves. "Yeah!"

Brandon laughed. He was itching to go outside, and with the coming of spring, the bluegill fish in Dad's large pond already had begun spawning.

Brandon rubbed his face. Cane pole fishing was also somewhat less painful as well.

BRANDON WAS the first out the homestead's back door. Upon leaving the canopy of the back porch, bright light greeted him, or more like assaulted him. He shut his eyes for a moment. "Ow! Thanks, sun."

After quickly fishing out his sunglasses from his khaki shorts pocket, Brandon could look around without the sunlight's interference. Even with as much land as his father owned, the forest still seemed to loom close due to the tall old trees beyond the Averys's property. It gave the land an almost magical feel.

Jubilee emerged from the doorway with her own

cane pole in hand. She had changed into a pair of jeans and a yellow T-shirt with faded dirt stains.

"You should have brought your gloves." Brandon chuckled. "You could have had a boxing match with the fish."

"Why fight an opponent who doesn't have a chance of winning?" Jubilee placed the pole over her right shoulder. "Besides, if I'm going to punch anything in the water, I want it to be a shark."

"Shark Puncher!" Brandon pointed to his sis. "That could be your ring name!"

The pair jogged out from under the shadow of their home. Brandon cast a departing look at the solar panels lining the roof, at the wind turbine that laid off to the side, gently spinning with the midmorning breeze, and at the small shed that housed a generator wired to their house. Up until the time Brandon had had friends over to the house, he never thought their setup was unusual. What, other people didn't generate their own electricity? Unbelievable! In the past few years, he had begun understanding how special his family was.

And how some people think we're oddballs, Brandon thought. That partially fueled Brandon's desire to indulge in the weird and the strange. He liked thinking of himself as apart from the rest of the human race. Which, given they lived such a self-sustained life out here, they probably were.

Soon they had raced past the line of crops and made it to the pond close to the west border of the

Avery lands. The pond's water fluttered slightly as soft wind blew over the surface.

Brandon fitted the string to his pole. The cane poles easily would drop their lures into the pond. The two of them wouldn't have to do anything other than sit there and wait for a bite from the bluegill fish below.

Oddly, Jubilee's attention was not fixed on the pond. She was staring off into the wooded lands beyond.

"Jubes?" Brandon asked, "What is it?"

His sister looked like a wary animal scouting the land for prey. Brandon had seen her like this before when Dad had taken them into the woods. Did she suspect there was trouble out there? The tall fence that lay a short distance away should be enough to keep away predators.

"I thought I saw something fly through the air," Jubilee said, "I barely saw it." She turned away. "Maybe it was nothing."

"You got jittery over a bird?" Brandon asked.

"I don't know." Jubilee shrugged. "It didn't look like a bird. It...oh, forget it."

Brandon turned back to the pond. Jubilee was worrying over nothing. What could happen here?

JACOB WAITED until his two children reached the pond before he turned back to the table with coffee in his hand. When the sound of his daughter's punches died down, Jacob figured a trip to the pond was almost inevitable. The children's time outside would keep things quiet around here for a while.

He sat down at the table where his wife waited for him. She wiggled her finger in the air. "I see a white hair."

Jacob sat down. "Liar," he said. After setting down his coffee, he ran a hand through his very short hair. Even in the sunlight pouring through the window, it was tough to tell if his hair was whitening. "If you really wanted to remind me of my age, you'd just talk my ear off about your plans for Jubilee's sixteenth birthday party."

"Oh, is that coming up?" Domino raised her head and looked away. Jacob chuckled at Domino's mock display of ignorance.

Jacob sat down, maneuvering his coffee so it did not sit on one of the catalogs littering the table. "Boy, this place is messy."

"Well, somebody needs to make time to go through these." Domino dangled one of the catalogs from her fingers. "I think this one is, what? Six years old?"

"It's not that old."

Domino playfully tossed it at him. "Whatever. You're a pack rat. You're afraid you'll see something you like and that you won't get a chance to order it again if you throw out the catalog."

Jacob sipped from his drink. The mess of catalogs

before them had served as their pipeline for all the things they could not procure from their life in the foothills of the Blue Ridge Mountains. The catalogs were not large, but thanks to Jacob's delays in going through them, they had piled up.

As Jacob pushed aside a pair of catalogs, his fingers grazed an open envelope containing a letter that he absolutely would have disposed of if it was not important. He couldn't hide a glare at the envelope.

Domino caught his gaze of anger. "Cowell doesn't have anything on us, Jacob." She leaned a little closer. "He's just a pain in the ass."

Jacob gripped one of the catalogs. "A pain in the ass who could cause us to lose our children."

"Like I said, he doesn't have anything on us," Domino replied.

Jacob clutched the catalog tighter. "He keeps claiming we're shutting in our children, particularly Jubilee, that we're depriving her from interacting with other girls her age."

"That's bullshit," Domino said, "Has he seen Richland High? We had Jubilee in their extracurricular self-defense class last year. She'd still be there if it wasn't for budget cuts."

"I know that. I told him that and it went in one ear and out the other. His problem is with Jubilee's lack of close friends. She doesn't have a best friend, anyone she's close to. Her interests just aren't the same as other girls."

"Jay, all girls are different. Even the ones who look and sound alike. Nobody can judge her because she hasn't found her..." Domino chuckled. "...her 'pack' yet."

Jacob chuckled. "Pack? What, girls are like wolves now?"

"Sometimes." Domino wiggled her eyebrows before taking another sip.

Jacob's laughter quickly faded. "And then there's our homeschooling curriculum. He's been going after that too..."

Domino, setting down her coffee, interrupted him. "Our homeschool curriculum is fine. It's well within the state's standards. Don't worry about Cowell. We've raised our kids just fine. It's far better than bringing up our children in a neighborhood with graffiti on the walls and cursing and guns and drugs..." She sighed. "We built ourselves a nice, safe little world for our little ones. Who could be against that?"

Jacob smiled, though he knew their world wasn't quite "safe." They still had to deal with the occasional wild animal that encroached close to their lands. Their grounds also were not totally safe from human intruders, although those were far and few between.

"Hey." Jacob scooted his chair a little closer to Domino without hitting one of the table posts. "I have a wonderful idea. Tonight, we barbecue. Put the best meat on the grill. Add some corn and potatoes, and we'll have one hell of a party."

Domino laughed. "A barbecue is one hell of a

party for you now, huh?" She rose from her seat. "Me too."

Once upon a time, parties were pretty damn rough for me and you, weren't they? Jacob stood up and approached his wife, ready to kiss her. Indeed, life had been good to them. It had not come easy, but the results had been well worth it.

Before Jacob's lips could make contact with his wife's, a terrible scream tore through the air. It came through the window.

"My God!" Domino rose to her full height.

Jacob didn't need his wife to tell him who that was. "Jubilee!"

CHAPTER TWO

BRANDON WASN'T sure what had happened. Everything had been going so well, so peacefully. Now his sister was on the ground, screaming horribly. She wasn't hurt in the sense she was stung by a mosquito or had tripped, fell, and banged her leg. Jubilee's screams came from cries of agony.

A moment ago, Brandon and Jubilee had been sitting at the pond, looking at the tiny movements within the water. Tiny fish were swimming past, too small to bite onto the bait that hung from their cane poles. Every now and then, the two of them would point to a bigger fish swimming by. However, those fish were too far from the poles. Would one of them ever notice the bait?

However, their attention had been interrupted by a shuffling noise. The shuffling soon turned to crunching. He and Jubilee turned their heads toward the woods. "You hear that?" Brandon had asked.

Jubilee raised her arms in a fighting stance. She was not someone to shy away from danger, but her widening eyes told Brandon that even she would not stick around if it was too dangerous.

"Someone's out there," she had said with a hushed whisper.

"Shit," Brandon had replied.

Jubilee had shot him a glare. "You know Mom doesn't like it when you say bad words."

Brandon had picked up some bad words, sometimes from Dad, though his father tried his best not to say anything he did not want his kids to repeat. But after accidently striking his thumb with a hammer, could anyone really blame Dad for saying what came next?

"Yeah, yeah, I know," he had replied to his sis.

"Let's bug out. It's hard to see with those trees hanging over the fence. Somebody could be out there, and we won't see them." Brandon had narrowed his eyes to look. "Like a skilled ninja assassin."

"Brandon, ninjas aren't going to attack us. This is for real." Jubilee had begun her jog down the dirt path that led back to the house. "C'mon!"

And then she fell to the ground with a loud scream.

"Jubes!" Brandon dropped to the dirt. Blood leaked down her right upper arm. "Are you shot?" Brandon's voice squeaked. Then he noticed the wooden arrow sticking out of her flesh.

The crunching sounds grew louder. They soon turned to rapid footfalls. Brandon spun his head around. Someone was approaching.

JACOB BURST out the front door with Domino just behind. His heart raced. That scream was blood curdling. He feared what had happened to his daughter. But what could have transpired out there? He had secured his property with a strong, tall fence. Predators could not get onto his land without some warning. And as for human intruders...

You've dealt with them before, Jacob thought. He had chased them off his land. And if they were hunting on his land, there was the chance his daughter had been caught in the crossfire.

"Jubilee!" Jacob cried as he raced past his crops toward the small hill just before his pond. "I'm coming!"

Once he crossed the hill, he had arrived at the pond. Jubilee was lying on the ground with Brandon standing over her. The boy was facing off against a tall man with a camouflage shirt, baggy pants and paint-stained boots. The man was holding an arrow and a bag over his shoulder. However, he was also sweaty, wide-eyed and shaking a little. He seemed more petrified than Brandon, whose fists were clenched and who looked ready to belt this guy hard.

"You son of a bitch! You shot my sister!" Brandon shouted.

"Whoa, wait! I'm just trying to help her. Yeah, it was all a mistake!" He started hyperventilating. "Oh shit, oh shit, oh shit. I didn't mean to hit her!"

One look at the man's face instantly told Jacob who he was. "Cribber," he said under his breath.

Cribber. Jacob had a word for guys like him—"douchebag outdoorsmen." They were the loser version of rural dwellers, not men who grew up in a culture of responsibility, knowing how to handle weapons and to obey the land laws, but amateurs who staggered onto his land and fired their arrows from bows like they were shooting foam objects from children's toys. In Jacob's mind, they were the rural versions of the punks who used to live in Jacob's neighborhood. Cribber might not be the dumbest of such guys, but he was close.

"Jubilee! My God!"

Domino knelt down next to her and tilted her right arm up. Blood trickled down from the arrow wound. Jubilee's eyes fluttered. She was going in and out of consciousness.

"Mom...Mommy..." the teen muttered.

"An arrow," Jacob whispered.

He didn't need further explanation. He knew what this shithead had done. He was trespassing—again—on his land and shooting at random birds and animals. Jacob had chased off Cribber and a fellow wanna-be hunter named Shellie. At least this time Cribber was alone.

"Whoa! Hey, Mister, uh, Avery. Look, I didn't even see where that arrow went." Cribber pointed to the sky. "I was aiming at a hawk. Going to mount him on my wall, you know." He chuckled. "Mount him with his wings out so it looks like he's going to fly down and shit, but he's really not, you know?"

"A hawk," Jacob said under his breath. "That's why you shot my daughter?" His voice exploded. "For a goddamned hawk?"

Cribber waved his hands. "Whoa! Like I said, I wasn't aiming at her. Hey, I didn't even see the bitch."

If Cribber had thought to apologize for calling Jubilee a bitch, he had no time to speak it. Jacob seized Cribber by the front of his camo shirt and head butted him in the nose.

Cribber screamed. Blood ran down from nostrils. It soon stained his shirt. He also dropped his bag of arrows and his bow onto the dirt.

"And that's just for starters," Jacob said, seething. He punched Cribber's nose a second time, flinging blood off onto the grass. Cribber screamed again.

"Hey! What's your blood doing on my grass?" Jacob asked, with a hint of sarcasm. "Your filth doesn't belong on my property!" Then he drove a knee into Cribber's chest.

"My land is too good for douchebags like you." With that, Jacob opened his hand and released Cribber, who promptly fell onto the ground, clutching his chest and whimpering.

"You know, I think you'd enjoy being at the bottom of my pond. It's a nice safe place. Oh, and I'm sure no one would think to look for you there. Actually, I don't think there's anyone who would want to look for you. You're a piece of garbage. Who would even give a shit about you?"

Crying, Cribber finally said after all the beating, "Look, man, give me a break!"

"A break?" Jacob cracked his right knuckles. "Oh, by all means, I'll give you—"

"Jay!" Domino cried.

Jacob stopped. His boot nearly stepped on Cribber's bow. He turned to his wife, who seemed agonized by the whole scene. "Please, worry about your daughter. Forget about him."

Jacob looked down at the bow. He stomped on it once -- hard. It cracked loudly under Jacob's boot. Meanwhile, Cribber climbed to his feet, still dribbling blood. Jacob did not advance on Cribber any longer.

"You...you're batshit crazy!" With that, Cribber ran off toward the woods.

Jacob let him go, but not without shouting, "If you come back here, I will run your head down into my pond and let my catfish eat your balls off!"

"Jay!" Domino grabbed him by the shoulders. "Please, forget him. Jubilee!"

The mention of his daughter's name snapped him

out of the remainder of his fury. What was Jubilee's condition?

He ran up to his girl. Domino already had broken off the arrow shaft and discarded it, but the arrow point itself was missing. It must be embedded in her skin. Jacob's stomach churned. For the moment, Brandon was pressing a cloth upon the wound to stop the bleeding.

"My God," Jacob said, "we have to get her to a hospital."

His eyes met Domino's. "Sheryl."

"But that's far," Domino protested.

"Two hours. But we don't have a choice. We need a good surgeon, and the best I know is my older sis. She'll be on duty for the next few hours. This..." He grimaced as he looked at Jubilee's arm again. "This looks pretty bad. We need to go. Now!"

JACOB REACHED the black pickup truck near the back of his home, at the entrance to his garage. It was rare for them to take a trip into the metro area of Washington D.C., but today the journey was vital. He wouldn't take his family there unless he didn't have any other choice. The Richmond metro area was too far, and Jacob did not know any surgeons in nearby towns that could handle a wound like Jubilee's. He had to go with a sure thing here.

Sheryl. God, this is going to be strange, barging in on you like this.

He hopped into the driver's seat and started the ignition. The vehicle smoothly hummed to life. Jacob personally had maintained this vehicle and even made special modifications. It would not fail him and his family today. Jacob had built in some fail-safes that would see to that.

Jacob drove the truck down a small driveway onto the dirt road that ran through his property. With a left turn, Jacob was now on grassy land near the pond. After stopping the truck close to his family, he jumped out and rejoined them.

"All right. Let's help her inside," Jacob said as he dashed to the truck's bed, which was shielded with a Diamond Back cover. Jacob yanked off the cover. Jacob would have taken a moment to feel satisfaction for how he had stocked his truck, but with his daughter hurt, he had to put his hard work into action.

He had outfitted his truck like a military equipment carrier. The bed was divided into numbered compartments. The compartment in the bed's center contained a large red backpack. Red was appropriate, for it was the color of first aid. This pack held enough supplies to help Jubilee through the next couple of hours.

He hurried to Jubilee with the pack, who by now was resting in the back seat. Jacob unzipped the pack and started fishing out supplies.

"Get the wound as clean as you can," Jacob said. As Domino worked on Jubilee's wound, Jacob added, "The arrowhead is going to have to come out, but we can't do that here."

"Right," Domino said.

Brandon had calmed down somewhat, but the boy still was a little jittery. Totally understandable after all he had been through.

"Brandon, get your get home bag. Have it with you, just in case," Jacob said.

Brandon snapped his hand into a salute before running to the truck bed. Giving him something to do would help calm him further. Jacob just hoped this was the sole emergency for the day.

GET YOUR GET HOME BAG. Brandon rarely had heard his father tell him to do that. He understood why, though. This was a long trip, and it paid to be ready.

Brandon climbed up on the truck's hanging tailgate. Once there, he reached out for the compartment that was numbered zero. It was strange to have a compartment labeled with a zero, but his dad insisted on it. Zero was an important number, one that inherently seemed alarming. Zero was the final number in a countdown. Zero was part of the phrase "ground zero." The very number denoted absolutely nothing, a void, an absence of any amount.

So, ironically, compartment zero held the family's

get home bags. Four backpacks lay nestled inside, each labeled with a single name: *Jacob, Domino, Jubilee, Brandon*.

Brandon grabbed the one with his name on it. He didn't have to check inside to know what the bag contained. The boy pictured its contents—a change of clothes, a light tarp, energy bars, water, first aid kit, a flashlight, batteries, a map, a compass, and a face mask--virtually everything Brandon would need to get him through a rough situation.

Brandon turned the bag on its side. It also contained a firearm, which was bound to the bag by MOLLE webbing. It was a stark reminder that these bags were not frivolous items. A get home bag was exactly that, a bag of supplies to help get the wearer home—by any means.

A sudden rustle caused Brandon to whip his head around. A crow flew past. He exhaled nervously. Cribber's actions had caused his heart to race whenever an unexpected noise cut through the air. He needed some reassurance. He wished he had super vision like a cyborg.

Or, he could just use his binoculars!

He unzipped the middle compartment. Dad had told them to keep binoculars in their bags so they could be on the lookout for bad actors. Brandon removed his and hung them around his neck. Now no hunter would sneak up on them!

After holstering his pack, Brandon hurried back to his family. Domino was scooting in the back to sit next to Jubilee. Brandon put the binoculars to his face and scanned the driveway in front of the house.

To his shock, the driveway was occupied by a visitor.

"Dad!" Brandon cried out, "Dad, come here! We got company!"

"Company?" Jacob joined his son. "Who could be coming over?" Jubilee's trainer wasn't coming in today, and if any of their friends were stopping by, they generally would have called ahead.

"It's him!" Brandon handed Jacob the binoculars. "Mister Cowell!"

CHAPTER THREE

JACOB'S HANDS clenched the binoculars. This was not what he needed. It was as if Cowell had decided upon the worst time to appear. Here Jacob was, his daughter bleeding from an arrow in hcr arm and her father having just beat up the guy who shot her. Cribber's blood still was fresh on Jacob's grass. How was this going to look?

Keep calm, Jacob thought. *You're totally in the right here. That asshole shot your daughter. He deserved what he got. Cowell can't possibly blame you. You're the victim. No, Jubilee is.*

If a reasonable person was headed for his property, Jacob would agree. But Alexander Cowell was not a reasonable person, at least as far as Jacob was concerned. The social worker was suspicious of all "off the grid" types. In fact, he wasn't thrilled about the rustic life at all. He looked upon the countryside as a decaying facet of the United States that eventually would be overtaken by bustling cities and suburbs. If you wanted to live out here, you were a barbarian or a cultist.

So, Jacob did not expect any fair treatment from Cowell. The man was sure to view Jubilee's injury as the natural result of living out here and bring this matter before a court. And if he learned Jacob had beaten up Cribber, Cowell would take that as further evidence that Jacob was a man prone to violence and not to be trusted with his own children.

Jacob stormed back to his truck. "Hurry! We have to go. Now! Cowell's here."

"Shit!" Domino reached out and slammed the back passenger side door shut while Jacob rushed into the driver's seat. Brandon piled inside through the front passenger side door.

Through the side mirror, Cowell's car came to a stop at the outer fence. He was far away. In fact, he was nearly on the opposite side of the property, but if Jacob lingered for too long, Cowell was sure to spot them and demand an audience. Cowell likely would take a refusal as evidence that Jacob was hiding something.

"The back road," Jacob said as he turned the ignition key. "We'll take that, and then use it to get to Road 219."

He started up the truck, not caring if Cowell heard it. He always could make up a story later about what he was doing. The less Cowell actually saw, the better.

Jacob hit the gas. He sped down the driveway onto the dirt road that ran past the back of his crops. He had driven through the back of his property many times to transport building material for his fences as well as for his crops, but not recently. The dirt path was uneven and grown over in spots. Jacob really had to pay attention to discern where the actual road was, which wasn't easy with the adrenalin rushing through his body. He had to take Jubilee to the hospital while escaping Cowell. That was more than enough to rattle him.

The road turned left. Jacob turned with it. However, he expected the road to keep going and not lead right into a wooden fence. Jacob slammed on the brakes. The front bumper of his vehicle stopped inches short of the fence.

"Damn it!" Jacob released the wheel. His hands shook. "I forgot I put up that fence a few years ago." He opened the door and dove out of the truck. Of course he had. He had wanted to fence off his property to protect against animals and people like Cribber. He had forgotten that he actually succeeded in fencing off the very back of his land as well.

Even so, Jacob remembered he had installed a gate here as well. He still was transporting materials through here while he was erecting the fence.

"Gate! Gate! Where's the gate?" He ran along the fence, searching for anything, a lock, a set of hinges, anything to mark the gate's separation from the rest of the fence. Why couldn't he remember? Was he so terrified of Cowell and his daughter's injury that thinking straight just wasn't an option.

Finally, his hand grazed a solid brass hinge. Here it was! Jacob had located the gate's lock. One of the keys on his ring unlocked it with no problem.

"Dad!" Brandon shouted. The boy had left the truck and was pointing back the way they had come. "I think I see Cowell!"

Blood rushed Jacob's arms and face as he pushed open the gate. Had the bastard actually climbed over his fence to get onto his property? Jacob wouldn't put it past Cowell.

"Into the truck!" Jacob cried. Brandon obeyed, reaching his seat just as Jacob sat down on his. At least they had their way out. Jacob wasted no more time driving the truck through the gap.

Common sense told him to stop and shut the gate, but Brandon's warning kept his foot on the gas. He couldn't see Cowell through the rear-view mirror, but Jacob refused to take the chance that Cowell could approach them and demand they stop. He didn't want to confront Cowell face to face and be forced to show Jubilee with her arrow injury. Better to have plausible deniability.

Soon Jacob's fence was long gone. The truck sped down a dirt road that whipped through tall grass and sporadic trees. Cowell was no longer an immediate problem. Jacob now could focus on getting his little girl to a hospital.

Domino let out an anguished breath. "This has

been the worst day ever," she said as Jubilee moaned against her.

"What is Cowell's deal?" Brandon asked, "Why does he keep showing up?"

Jacob rubbed his lips together to burn off some frustration. "He believes he's protecting you from your psycho father," he said, juicing his words with sarcasm. "He doesn't care about anyone but his own ego."

"I think he's a cyborg in disguise." Brandon folded his arms. "He's from the future and he wants to kill us one day because we're destined to save the world."

Brandon's remark was almost enough to fully melt Jacob's anxiety and anger—almost. "Well," he finally said, "I can buy that he's not human."

Jubilee moaned again. "Mom...it hurts so bad."

"Speaking of the world," Domino said, "how about we put on the radio? Maybe it'll distract Jubilee until we reach the hospital."

Jacob switched on the radio. As the speakers crackled to life, the dirt road turned off onto Road 219. Jacob made the turn. Now they were truly on their way to Sheryl's hospital.

The radio had been tuned to a news talk station, so instead of music, a slightly gravel-throated male voice poured through the speakers.

"...so, this is definitely the first time the White House has expressed concern about the recent solar phenomenon. White House Spokesman Conrad Watters said the President has endorsed the McKinney-Shepherd bill that would upgrade the country's electrical grid. But some believe the government should have undertaken these measures as far back as last year, when telescopes first started detecting the solar bursts. But some in Congress still contend this is a waste of time and resources, and that most electrical grids are sufficiently hardened from solar activity."

Brandon groaned. "Bor-ing. Can we listen to music, please?"

Jacob obliged his son and turned on a classic rock station, slightly embarrassed that he had listened for so long. Then again, solar activity had blanketed the news for almost a year now. It was hard not to miss it.

DOMINO FLICKED a strand of hair out of Jubilee's face. "Hey. Hang in there. We won't be too much longer."

Jubilee nodded. "Thank you."

As long as the traffic doesn't get too bad, Jacob thought, though he kept his thoughts to himself. They were past lunch, so they should be past the lunch crowd. However, Jacob had heard news reports of construction activity in the area. If a lane or two was coned off, that could create a bottleneck and delay them considerably.

"How do you think we're going to explain this to

Aunt Sheryl?" Brandon asked, with a nervous laugh. "You know she thinks we're weird already."

Jacob shared Brandon's concern, if only slightly. Sheryl shared Jacob's dislike of the neighborhood they grew up in, but unlike Jacob, Sheryl prized education and career advancement as the way out of it. She thought Jacob's plan to relocate into the countryside was insane. She claimed repeatedly that Jacob did not have the skills to handle it. Jacob protested that he could learn. Sheryl believed Jacob, with his average-at-best school grades, should have sought something like a college degree in engineering to set him up. She feared that he would be a failure. Even now, she carried great doubts about Jacob's lifestyle, and the two had a bittersweet relationship as a result.

She still cares about my kids, Jacob thought. *She would do whatever it took to help them*.

"Hey Dad, we got trouble!" Brandon suddenly cried.

"Trouble? Where?" Jacob asked.

Brandon was looking at the side mirror attached to the right side of the truck. Jacob checked his rear-view mirror. Brandon was correct. Trouble was approaching in the form of Alex Cowell.

"Damn it!" Jacob squinted to be sure he wasn't seeing things. No, there was no mistake. Cowell's black four-door was far behind, resembling a large toy, but there was no doubt it was Cowell's vehicle, judging from the decaying paint job on the vehicle's roof.

"Cowell? How?" Domino asked.

"That's crazy!" Jubilee shouted before groaning in pain.

Jacob's mind raced. *How did Cowell catch up with them?* "The back road," he said, seething. "It's got a wide loop. It joins up with the highway, but it eats up a few miles to do it. Cowell could have checked out our place, got in his car, and drove up to the highway. Hell, he might have been lying in wait at the intersection!"

It seemed silly, but it was the only thing that made sense. If Cowell had left their home shortly after he arrived, he should have been out ahead of them, not behind. Cowell must have suspected that Jacob and his family had departed through the back and drove up to the turnoff to the highway to wait for Jacob's truck to pass.

"He really is a cyborg," Brandon said.

"Is he really going to follow us all the way to the hospital?" Domino asked.

"No doubt about it. He's hunting for our scalps."

Cowell seeing Jubilee would be incredibly bad, but Jacob also didn't want Cowell to talk to Sheryl. Cowell had been questioning people who knew the Averys, and more than once had expressed his desire to speak to Sheryl. It was part of the reason Jacob had urged Sheryl to steer clear of his house for a while. Sheryl thought Jacob was being a little paranoid, but Jacob believed the less Sheryl knew about his life, the better. It meant Sheryl would not be a credible witness for Cowell.

"We've got to get rid of him," Jacob said.

However, that might be easier said than done. The traffic on this highway still was light, so Jacob couldn't lose Cowell amid a sea of cars, and there were few alternative routes to Sheryl's hospital. It was not like Jacob easily could lose Cowell along the way.

"I have an idea." Jacob pressed on the gas. The speedometer roared to sixty miles per hour, then sixty-five, then seventy.

"Jay!" Domino cried.

"Don't worry! I just need to buy some time. Then you're going to take it from here."

ON THE SIDE of the road, very close to the painted white stripe that bordered the road's edge, Jacob waved the white towel high in the air. If he was right, Cowell would pass by any moment.

It didn't take long for Cowell's black car to approach. Jacob stepped out into the lane, waving the towel even faster. Cowell slowed his vehicle until it halted a few paces from Jacob.

Gotcha, Jacob thought.

Cowell turned off the car's ignition. The driver's side door opened. Jacob waited. His plan was working perfectly. Now he simply had to deal with the man who was exiting the vehicle.

Alex Cowell would have been shorter than Jacob except for his well-heeled shoes. The man's brown jacket appeared a dingy yellow in this sunlight, which almost made Jacob laugh. But humor seemed to be an alien concept to Cowell. The man's stone face was made more implacable by his reddish-brown beard and dark glasses. With his white shirt, blue tie, and dark brown pants, the man was the picture of the bureaucratic professional. How this guy got to be a social worker, Jacob could not say. He projected no warmth and, in all of Jacob's experiences, slighted the life that Jacob and his wife chose to lead.

Cowell slowly approached Jacob with all the grace of a police officer who just had pulled over a speeding motorist. "Mister Avery," he said, "well, isn't it interesting to suddenly meet you out here in the middle of the road?"

"I thought I'd go for an afternoon jog," Jacob said. "It's quite nice out here."

"Really? If I didn't know any better, I'd think you were avoiding me."

Jacob grinned. "Well, talking with you is the highlight of any day, Mister Cowell."

"Where's your family? You're not fooling me, Avery. You were in your truck. You must have pulled over for some reason."

"Actually, they've gone on ahead. They're pressed for time. If you had something very important you wanted to speak to me about, well, I thought I'd go ahead and meet up with you so we can chat."

"Cute. Real cute." Cowell's lips curled into a snarl while saying "cute." "I told you I'd be in touch regarding your children."

"Yes, but such visits generally require the courtesy of a phone call, don't they?" Jacob put as much sarcasm into his voice as he could. "You seem to think you can show up on my lawn any time you want."

"There's nothing wrong with a surprise visit, Mister Avery. It's to make sure you're not putting on a show for my benefit. Some people have expressed concerns about your children, particularly your daughter's current state, and I aim to make sure she is not being unlawfully deprived or detained on your property."

"Really?" Jacob tried swallowing his anger. "You know, all my friends, doctors, people who I talk to say you're, well, pushy with your questions. You throw out accusations instead of trying to get to the truth, and you lead people on to hunt for the answers you want."

"You can call it whatever you like. I will, however, speak to your daughter and son."

"Fine, schedule an appointment. We'll do lunch."

"Where are they, Mister Avery? I'm beginning to suspect something's amiss. Is your daughter quite alright?"

Jacob's anger threatened to boil over. "Mister Cowell," he said through grinding teeth, "Do you have a court order in those fancy clothes of yours to come into my home and talk to my family? Because if you don't have a legal basis to talk to my kids, you're going to have to go through the law of the magic word."

Cowell frowned. "Magic word?"

Jacob nodded. "Please." He advanced one step on Cowell and said with a little mockery, "Mister Avery, may I please speak with your children at a convenient time?"

Now Jacob's mood was improving. Cowell just stood there like a statue. Jacob was enjoying this.

"If you don't, I might just go to court and start throwing words around like 'stalking' and 'harassing.' And then you may hear the word 'fired' from your bosses soon afterward. You know, there are groups out there who don't take to the government harassing people who live off the grid. I don't think your bosses want the publicity."

Cowell chortled. "You're not nearly as clever as you imagine yourself to be, Mister Avery. There are people who knew you back when you were younger. Seems you weren't exactly an angel." He backed up toward his car. "Make no mistake, there is a substantial case against you. All you have to do is mess up just once, and you'll have that court order. No, you'll be *in* court yourself."

Cowell climbed back into his car and started up the motor. With a hearty sigh, Jacob wiped his face with the white towel. He did it. Cowell could not hope to catch up to his family now, even if he knew where they were going.

As Cowell started up his car, Jacob fished out his cell phone. He would not ask his wife to turn around and pick him up. None of his friends were nearby. Hey, maybe he could dial an Uber driver. He never had done that before. Could be interesting.

Before he could look up Uber, he heard a car engine suddenly begin puttering out. Cowell's car was decelerating rapidly. The brake lights weren't even on. It was as though someone had pulled the plug on Cowell's vehicle.

Jacob scratched his head. Cowell's car had come to a complete halt. He obviously had suffered a breakdown, perhaps due to a bad battery.

"Just my damn luck," Jacob said as he returned his attention to his phone. He still planned to call that Uber driver, although with Cowell stopped close by, he might receive another earful from the social worker while he waited.

However, Jacob's phone was dead. The screen was black. Jacob tapped it several times, to no avail.

"What the hell?" Jacob whispered.

CHAPTER FOUR

THOUGH DOMINO's eyes remained on the highway ahead of them, she couldn't help but glance back at the cell phone in Brandon's hand. It had not stirred in the past twenty minutes.

She shouldn't be so nervous. Her husband could deal with Alex Cowell. The important thing was to get Jubilee to Sheryl's hospital. If Jacob was successful, he might be able to drive Cowell away for the rest of the day.

She glanced at her daughter in the back. She was awake, but clearly miserable. Her lip was curled up and she kept a hand on her wound.

Silence was out of the question. Domino had to keep everyone's spirits up and Jubilee's thoughts off her ordeal. "Hey! Roddie in the afternoon's coming on. He's going to be talking about the MMA fight this weekend." She turned to Jubilee. "Bet you're going to love that, huh?"

Jubilee smiled weakly. "Sure."

Brandon switched on the radio. But instead of Roddie's all-too excited voice spilling from the speakers, the trio was treated to a news broadcast in progress.

"...as a result of the sudden increase in solar activity. Also, it is estimated that forty thousand passengers have cancelled their flights amid news that the government will order flights to be grounded. The White House insists this is a precautionary move and there is no actual threat to air flight operations. There is also a sudden rush on faraday cages. Sales have been robust in the past few months, but with today's news, sales have skyrocketed."

Jubilee groaned. "We can't get away from this!"

Domino switched the channel to a music station, which was also overlaid with the same news broadcast. "Damn. This is serious," she said.

"They're worried about electromagnetic disruptions in the atmosphere," Brandon said, his tongue nearly tripping over the word 'electromagnetic.'

"But what does that mean?" Jubilee cried out. It was painful, but she stifled it so she could speak further. "I understand what 'electromagnetic' means, but why is everyone making it such a big deal?"

Domino studied the traffic outside as she answered. The lanes were starting to fill up. "Well, baby, a solar burst in the atmosphere sends out electromagnetic pulses. The government is just worried that if those pulses are too strong, they can damage power grids. They also can shut down electronic devices." Domino pointed to her phone in Brandon's hand. "Like phones."

"Hey, maybe we should call Aunt Sheryl to let her know we're coming," Brandon said.

"Yeah, that's a good idea. If it's not your dad talking to her, it'll go easier," Domino said.

"Why...do they...hate each other?" Jubilee asked through her moans.

"They don't hate each other. They're just a little awkward around each other. They're very different people," Domino responded.

"Hey, what's her phone number?" Brandon asked.

"Open the glove compartment," Domino said, "your dad taped the phone number inside it."

Brandon opened the compartment. At the same time, Domino spotted a slow-moving car and applied the brakes.

Suddenly, anything that was lit up on the dash-board, from the gauges to the radio, winked out, along with the truck's engine. Domino gasped. "Holy shit!" She pumped the brakes again. She was coasting right toward the back of that car at about forty miles per hour!

Facing an imminent collision, Domino turned right. The truck sped off the road into the tall grass, barely avoiding a speed limit sign in the process, while still trying to pump the brakes. Their seat belts held them in their seats, though not without some jostling as the truck made the jump off the road. The truck skidded and shuddered through the grass until Domino's constant jamming on the brakes brought the vehicle to a stop.

"Holy shit!" Brandon said.

Domino nearly scolded her son for using a curse word, but she was too stunned to make the rebuke.

"Mom! What happened?" cried Jubilee.

Domino turned the key in the "off" position, then turned it back on. Nothing. The engine was dead.

"I don't know. Everything's dead." Domino turned to Jubilee. "Are you okay?"

Jubilee fingered her belt. "I didn't hit anything."

"That was almost fun," Brandon said with a laugh.

Domino unbuckled herself. "The battery must have died. I'm going to try the backup generator Jacob packed in the bed."

DOMINO WORKED QUICKLY, opening up the back bed, accessing the generator and connecting it to the truck's battery. But the generator did not switch on. Nothing Domino did coaxed the generator to life.

"Are you kidding me?" Domino was so startled she nearly hit her head on the underside of the hood. The generator was less than a year old. Even the battery was only two years old. How could both the battery and the generator be out?

"Mom!" Jubilee called from the truck. The back door was open. The teen still sat in her seat, holding her phone with her shaky left hand. "My phone doesn't work."

"Your phone's dead as a brick, too." Brandon, walking outside the truck, raised the phone to his mom's eyes, showing a completely dark screen.

Domino's mouth gaped open. The truck battery, the backup generator, and all their phones? This was unbelievable.

I was just talking about solar activity with the kids. A cold shudder ran all the way down to her feet. There was no way all of their electronics could be busted.

Then she realized she had not paid any attention to the highway. She had been too wrapped up in trying to restart the truck. After turning her gaze to the road, her worst fears were confirmed.

The road was a mess of stopped vehicles from one horizon to the other. It was as if someone had pressed a pause button on a cosmic remote control and frozen everything in place. Domino then noticed that not all the vehicles smoothly stopped. There were at least three rear-end collisions and two more had sped off the highway just as Domino had done.

Brandon crept up to Domino. "Mom." He sounded quieter, almost younger.

He's afraid, Domino thought. *I understand how he feels*.

COWELL WOULDN'T STOP POKING at his phone. "I

cannot believe this!" He looked up from his car. He had fed his phone into the car's cigarette lighter, but it had done nothing to rejuvenate it.

"It's no use," Jacob said. "Face it, it's all dead."

"Both my phone and my car?" Cowell scowled. "Ridiculous."

"My phone's dead, too. Whether we like it or not, this is much bigger than just a simple car breakdown. It's a phenomenon, something that's hit a wide area."

"Phenomenon. What nonsense." Cowell climbed back into his car. He had discarded his brown jacket on the passenger seat. Without his air conditioner, he was increasingly uncomfortable in the heat. "There is a perfectly logical explanation for this. Someone will be along and will tell us."

Jacob gazed at the road. Nobody had driven along since Cowell's car had stopped. "Look, you can do what you want, but I have to catch up with my family. If I run into police, a tow truck, somebody, I'll be sure to tell them about you."

"Don't think this is going to change my opinion of you," Cowell replied. "Once this...whatever is going on here... once it's over, I will be interviewing your children."

Jacob started walking. "Just watch out for the wolves out there!"

"Wolves? This is Virginia, not Arizona!" Cowell barked at him. A few steps later, Cowell added, "A pathetic attempt at a joke, Mister Avery! I'll remember it!"

Jacob shook his head. "Maybe I should worry more about the animals if they run into him," he muttered.

IT DIDN'T TAKE LONG before Jacob ran across another car. Like Cowell's, it was stopped dead in the right lane. The driver, standing by his open hood, looked at the engine inside with wide eyes and an open mouth.

So, Cowell's not the only one to break down? No doubt about it, something had shut down electronic devices in this area.

Jacob approached the driver and began chatting with him. The man was understandably frazzled. Additionally, his phone had gone dead at the same time that his car lost power.

Jacob explained to the man that he was going to seek help. The motorist understood and said he would wait by his car. Jacob then continued his journey up the highway.

A few minutes later, things grew worse in a hurry.

The highway was cluttered with stopped or crashed automobiles. Drivers were milling about on the road, talking to each other, exchanging questions, concerns and theories.

Worry was filling Jacob's mind. There was no way Domino and the children could have reached the hospital before the truck stalled. The mystery phenomenon surely had caught them as well.

"Shit!" Jacob broke into a run. What if they had collided with another car or something that wouldn't give? A horrible image of his truck smashed like an accordion seized his thoughts.

My God. If I hadn't let them go on ahead of me, if I was behind that wheel instead of Domino...

However, a fast run down the highway wasn't in the cards. The mess of the stopped or crashed cars forced Jacob to weave through the mess carefully. Every now and then somebody would ask him for answers or help or anything. Jacob had to politely but quickly urge them to let him pass.

I shouldn't be too scared. We prepared. Yeah, we prepared for emergencies like this. If they are still with the truck, they should have everything they need...

DOMINO PULLED out her get home bag. She thought she might need it in case of a sudden storm or terrorist attack. She never imagined she would have to use it because the sun decided to pull the plug on everything electronic.

If it was the sun. Domino had learned the sun was not the sole source of a devastating EMP. A nuclear weapon, detonated at a high altitude, could generate the same kind of pulse. But if it was a nuke, then that meant the country was at war, and might be on the losing end of it.

Domino next removed Jubilee's bag. She urged her daughter to remain in her seat. The open truck doors kept the air circulating as much as possible.

"Mom." Brandon slipped on his pack. "What are we going to do? If the cars don't work anymore, how is Dad going to find us?"

"Knowing him, he'll be hiking this way. He should run into us." Domino checked the direction from where they had come. Still no sign of him. "We probably should walk back the other way and try meeting him."

"Mom..." Jubilee huffed. Her breathing sounded a little more labored. Without the air conditioner, the injured girl was gulping in hot outside air. In her state, it had to be taking a toll on her. God only knew how she could talk amid the searing pain in her arm.

Domino cringed. "God, I don't even know if you can walk. A doctor. Maybe there's a doctor out here who can do something for you."

It sounded like a ridiculous hope. There were probably no more than thirty people milling about the highway. What were the odds that any of them was a practicing doctor?

Still, Domino asked around. To her disappointment, but not to her surprise, she didn't find a doctor among the stranded motorists. Not even a nurse.

Dejected, Domino staggered back to the truck. "I guess that was too much to hope for."

"But we have to help Jubilee. Can we still make it to the hospital?" Brandon asked.

Domino grimaced. "If the power's out there, it's going to be much, much worse. You're going to have tons of people outside trying to get answers. It's going to be a boiling pot of problems." Then she clutched her chest. "Sheryl. Oh my God. She's there in the middle of it all."

"Mom, I don't feel very good," Jubilee said.

Her options were almost nil. Meeting back up with Jacob seemed like the only possible course of action

"Excuse me." Domino turned around.

A middle-aged woman came strolling over to her. "I overheard you asking about a doctor. What's the problem?" Then she noticed Jubilcc and her wound. "Holy mother of God. No wonder you're looking for a doc."

"Yeah, and we really could use one ASAP, but it seems like the world just decided to go to Hell on us," Domino said with a nervous laugh.

"Well, I know of one doctor who is close enough if you're walking. He's Doc Sam. Lives in Trapp. Helped me out once. He's a stand-up guy. He can help your little lady, but you may want to get going soon."

"Doc Sam," Domino repeated. She never had heard of him. "Can you give me an address? I can't Google anybody right now."

"Sure. Got a pen and paper?"

Brandon dug out a pad from the truck and wrote down Doc Sam's address along with directions to get there and to get to Trapp from their current location. Domino thanked the woman before she left.

Brandon nearly tripped while carrying the folded-out map. He had retrieved it from the truck's glove compartment. "Trapp's still going to be a little while if we have to walk there."

"It's our best shot," Domino said as she brought Jubilee her bag. She took it but didn't look very enthusiastic about their impending journey.

Domino helped Jubilee out of the truck. Her legs quaked, and it took a moment for her to steady herself.

"Alright." Domino looked back to the road. Still no sign of Jacob. "We can't just go off without your father. He'll never know where to look for us."

"We could leave a note in the truck," Brandon said.

"Sweetie, I don't want to take that chance. Someone might steal it. You don't know what kind of nuts are going to be out here now that things have gone south." But as Domino looked at her daughter's pale face, she wondered how much longer she could stick around here.

"Hey!" Brandon plastered the map against the side of the truck. "Check this out." He pointed to a canal that jetted across the highway. "This is back the way we came, and it leads right to Trapp. If we hurry, we probably could meet Dad before he gets there!"

JACOB WIPED fresh sweat from his head. He had to be closing in on his family. There was no way they could be much farther. If the truck skidded to a stop, he should spot it soon. He remained furious, though, at all the delays he had experienced along the way. He could not blame the stranded motorists for looking for help, but he constantly had to explain that he had no supplies on his person and didn't know where to find help.

As the minutes wore on and he encountered more stalled vehicles without spotting a single operating one, his personal dread increased. Anything strong enough to knock out this many cars and take out electronics was unusually powerful. It couldn't be localized to just this part of Virginia. Hell, it might be nationwide, or even worldwide.

If it's that bad, then no help is coming.

First thing's first. He had to locate his family. The future meant nothing if he faced it without his loved ones.

At this point, the highway extended across an overpass that overlooked an irrigation canal. The overpass was clear of cars. Thankfully, none had stalled here. However, it was not totally unoccupied. Three figures just now were stepping onto the overpass on the other side.

Jacob's eyes widened. One of the pedestrians was a woman. Another was a boy. The third limped along beside the female. That was a female teenager. Could they be?

"Domino," he said with a whisper. "Brandon." He started running. "Jubilee?"

His weariness from the past hour of walking did nothing to slow him down. He ran until he confirmed, to his great relief, that the three were indeed his family.

"Dad!" Brandon called. He extended his arms. Jacob quickly caught them and hugged his son.

Domino laughed. "Jay! Oh, thank God!" She bent over. Jacob quickly released Brandon. Domino was not only carrying her pack but Jacob's as well, and the toll had exhausted her. Jacob slipped the bag out of her hands and then hugged her.

"You're all safe," Jacob said through heavy breaths. After a protracted embrace, he turned to his daughter. He lightly held her by her back, avoiding her wound. Jubilee just lightly smiled. Otherwise, she looked dreadful. Her skin was pale, and her right arm even was turning a little green.

"Jay, we found out about a doctor." Domino pointed to the canal. "He's not far. We can make it, but Jubilee..."

"She looks too worn out. Don't worry. I'll carry her all the way. I don't care how far it is."

"The doctor's in Trapp," Brandon said.

"Good. I know that town." Jacob looked down at Brandon. "You think you can carry my stuff?"

Brandon snapped his hand into a salute. "You bet."

A soft rustling turned Jacob's head. Someone was in the area, and Jacob frowned when he identified the visitor. Alexander Cowell was approaching across the bridge.

CHAPTER FIVE

"I DON'T BELIEVE THIS," Domino said.

"Easy," Jacob replied, "He's in the same boat as everyone else. He broke down shortly after we had our little talk."

Cowell was staggering. Jacob figured the man was not used to long walks, and the bitterness on the man's face confirmed the social worker's sour mood. His tie was gone, and his shirt was unbuttoned down to the middle to expose a white undershirt. Spots of dirt coated his neck and face, possibly blown onto him by the wind.

The closer he approached, the more Jacob could hear his heavy breathing. Cowell locked eyes with Jacob from several paces away. This guy was pissed. Jacob made a mental note to watch himself. Cowell had been content to throw his weight around as long as he thought he had the power of the law behind him, but how would he act if he realized he did not possess that power any longer?

"So, here's the whole Avery flock," he said as he slowed down and took a look at each member of the family. When he spotted Jubilee, his eyes widened a tad. "What's this? What's wrong with your daughter?"

"She was hit with an arrow. A hunter who had no business being on my property was shooting arrows and one hit her," Jacob replied.

"Is that so? So, your daughter was struck by Robin Hood, is that it?"

"The damned arrowhead is still in her arm. I'm trying to get her to a doctor to get it taken out," Jacob replied.

"Then why didn't you call thc policc?" Cowell turned to Jacob. "This is a criminal offense. Your alleged shooter should be in custody by now."

Jacob admitted silently that Cowell had a point. If he had been thinking clearly, he would have called the police instead of pounding Cribber with his own fists. He had lost his head, plain and simple, though he also would argue that since his daughter was attacked, he had a right to respond in self-defense.

Admittedly, it was a stretch. But Jacob was used to fending for himself. That included defending his family and property without relying on law enforcement.

"Well?" Cowell asked.

"I don't have time to play games with you. My

daughter is hurt. That wound can become infected if it isn't already. I have to act fast," Jacob said.

"As I thought. Why do I feel you're covering up a stupid accident that took place on your property? No wonder you tried to keep me from trailing your family." Cowell wiped sweat from his face. "I warned you against messing up. Well, you have messed up in spades. I will definitely have a court order to have your family investigated. You can expect to have a judge breathing down your neck—"

"Really?" Now Jacob could not take it any longer. "When do you think the courthouse is going to be open? Tomorrow? Next week? Do you realize what the hell just happened?"

"Evidently some kind of storm has broken out, something I'm sure will be explained when the authorities let us know."

"Well, it's probably going to be a long wait." Jacob eyed the skies. "I hope to God I'm wrong."

"Jay," Domino began.

"I know. You're thinking the same thing, too." Jacob turned from Cowell, back to his family. "So, looks like we're headed for Trapp. But the only turnoff I know that gets us there is back that way." He pointed to the road behind him, over Cowell's shoulder.

"I know how to get there!" Brandon pointed down the canal. "That way! It won't take long."

"Just a moment, Mister Avery. It sounds as if you're taking a chance with your daughter."

Cowell advanced on them, so close he nearly butted in between Jacob and his wife. The near intrusion caused Jacob to clench a fist. This guy was overstepping his boundaries, and Jacob would not hesitate to let him know.

"You ought to be looking for a clinic, someplace reputable, or somewhere like a police station where they can get in touch with a doctor," Cowell said.

"I will deal with this in my own way. Now do us a favor and get the hell away from us," Jacob said with all the calm he could muster. Then he crouched down, allowing Jubilee to climb onto his back.

"Wait!" Cowell waved his hand at the packs on Brandon's and Domino's backs. "You have packs. Did you know about this?"

"We prepared. We never took anything for granted." Jacob started walking across the overpass.

"Don't walk away!" Cowell shook his finger at them. "I want answers! What did you know about this? What's going to happen now? Damn you! You'll tell me what's going on here!"

THE AVERYS TREKKED alongside the canal with Jacob in the lead. The journey would have proceeded at a faster clip if the land was more level, but Jacob had to be cautious. One trip could not only send Jacob falling but Jubilee as well.

The group had remained quiet this whole time.

Perhaps it was weariness, or shock. Both Jacob and Domino suspected what had happened but did not want to voice it for fear of confirming what they believed.

It was hard, though, for Jacob to push his worries about the world aside. Every now and then he would gaze up at the sky. Usually, several times a day, he would hear a plane soaring overhead on their way to the airports in the D.C. area. That was not the case now. For the past couple of hours, he had not heard a thing overhead except the occasion cawing bird.

It wasn't long, however, before the end of their journey loomed in sight. A small town stretched out before them. The irrigation canal joined with a second one in a T-intersection. While the next canal seemed to bar their way to the town, an old wooden bridge across it instantly offered a solution. They would be in Trapp soon.

Soft crunching sounds drew Jacob's attention. Turning his head, he discovered that Cowell was trailing them from a distance. He was not making up much ground as he stepped gingerly, keeping his gaze mostly to the ground.

"Dad, the cyborg's back," Brandon said.

"I know," Jacob said, "he wants answers. He doesn't know what's going on and he thinks we do. He'd have left us behind if he did." He directed his attention forward. "Doms, keep an eye to our rear, just in case."

Domino, nodding, flashed an acidic look at the man following them.

As they crossed the bridge, an additional thought chilled his bones. His sister! She was in the D.C. area. She would be in the middle of a densely populated area with no electricity. Jacob had read studies on what would happen to society if there was a complete loss of power and electronics. It wasn't going to be pretty. The best bet in the initial aftermath would be to flee from any large population centers and find refuge out in the countryside or sparsely populated areas.

Sheryl, I gave you my address. If you're smart, you'll get the hell out of there!

He was so lost in his thoughts that he nearly bumped into the bridge's side barrier. He sucked in a heavy breath and kept going. Jubilee came first. Any worries about Sheryl would have to wait.

"THIS IS THE ADDRESS," Brandon said slowly. The disbelief in his voice was obvious. Jacob could understand why.

For one thing, the house that stood before them was the oddest house Jacob ever had seen. It was composed of white bags held together with barbed wire. The bags were thick. They would have to be to maintain the structure of this dwelling. But what the hell was in them?

"Dad?" Brandon asked.

"Yeah, I know." Jacob shook his head.

"Earthbags," Domino said, "there's got to be dirt or sand in them."

Jacob took a step closer. "I guess it'd have to be."

"So, this Doc Sam guy built his house out of sand?" Brandon asked.

"Don't knock it, Son. This might actually be cheaper than making it out of wood, cement and drywall," Jacob said with a slight laugh. But even so, what did this say about the man's ability to help Jubilee? Was this man too eccentric to help them out?

A closer look revealed that Doc Sam had taken some steps to secure his house. He had woven barbed wire to hold the bags together. The bags also were given an epoxy finish to help smooth the outer surface.

The immediate land surrounding the house looked about as strange. Cacti encircled the home. It was as if the home had been scooped up from a desert somewhere and dropped down into this grassy area.

"Domino, did that woman tell you anything about this Doc Sam?" Jacob asked.

Domino shook her head. "She just told me he could help. She didn't say anything else, even what he looked like. She definitely didn't tell me about all of this." She waved to the cactus plants.

Jubilee now was slumbering on Jacob's back. The

trip had exhausted her. "Here, help her off." Jacob crouched down. Brandon and Domino helped slide Jubilee off onto the grass.

With Jubilee down, Jacob stole a glance behind them. There was no sign of Alex Cowell. Their shadow evidently had decided to break off upon entering Trapp. Good. He did not want that man on his mind while he was trying to secure Doc Sam's help.

"What are we going to do?" Brandon asked.

Jacob steadied himself. He was exhausted himself from the long walk and carrying Jubilee. He fought the urge to sit down and rest. If there was a legit doctor in that house, he had to convince him to help his daughter.

"I'm going to go knock on the door," Jacob replied to Brandon with mock casualness.

"Wait!" Domino drew the gun from Jacob's get home bag.

Jacob shook his head. "Great idea, Doms. I go to his house with a gun. What do you think he's going to do?"

"If he's not a maniac, fine. But if he is..."

"People who aren't maniacs might still jump the gun. I can't take that chance. Hold on to it for me."

JACOB APPROACHED the front door of the home. He looked around the door frame for cameras or peepholes. What should he do? Perhaps he ought to reveal that he wasn't armed. He held out his arms while keeping his hands open and kept that stance.

"Well? What do you want me to do, high-five you?" spoke a male voice from behind the door.

Jacob cleared his throat. "I, uh, just wanted to show that I don't have any weapons."

"Thanks, friend. Let me get my shotgun so I can blow you away without any recriminations while I rob you. You're a hell of a smart one. Why don't you just wear a sign that says 'I'm a dumbass?'"

Jacob's cheeks burned. "Sir, I was just trying to show I wasn't any threat to you."

"Well, that's stupid. If you're not a threat, then I could kill you on the spot."

"Sir, I don't have time to waste." Jacob lowered his arms. "My daughter's hurt. Are you Doc Sam?"

"Let me check my mirror." A brief pause. "Yeah, I'm still Doc Sam. Hold on a sec."

Jacob waited amid the sound of opening locks from the other side of the door. Then, once the door finally was pulled open, Jacob was greeted by the sight of a man whose appearance definitely matched the eccentricity of his home. The first thing Jacob noticed was the man's tremendous eyebrows. They spouted from his head like whiskers. Otherwise, he was clean shaven, and his head was shiny and bald. His upper body, however, belied his age. He was an active man, no question about it. He seemed pretty formidable for his age.

The man raised his eyebrows. "So, what happened?"

"My daughter was shot in the arm by some stupid guy who thought he was a hunter," Jacob said. "Please let me bring her inside. She needs help, quickly."

The doctor stepped past Jacob, stopping between two of his tallest cacti, a place where he could view Jacob's family easily. "I didn't expect you so soon," he said.

"So soon?" Jacob asked.

Doc Sam looked up at the blue sky. "The EMP. You know about it, right?"

"Of course. The damned thing stopped my truck. I had to hike all the way back to my family."

"I knew folks would be showing up here, but you all sure got here sooner than I figured," Doc Sam said.

Jacob scooped up Jubilee in his arms. "Guess we were just lucky."

"You may wish for all the luck you can get," Doc Sam said, a little more solemnly than before. "C'mon, let's get her inside."

CHAPTER SIX

Jacob carried his daughter into Doc Sam's home while Domino and Brandon waited outside. The living room was small, with a big couch, a smaller loveseat, several chairs, and an end table. There was no television set. The area reminded Jacob more of a waiting room.

A waiting room. So, this place might be the doctor's clinic after all. The overall interior was fascinating to look at. A wooden lattice held up walls and a ceiling. Doors led to other rooms, one behind Jacob and Jubilee, one off to the side, and a third which Doc Sam was opening up right at that moment.

Jacob followed. In this room, Jacob was greeted by a raised bed and a bevy of medical instruments.

"Put her there." Doc Sam jabbed his finger to the bed. The covering sheet was pulled back, allowing Jacob easily to deposit his daughter onto it. She moaned a bit but did not move. Jacob was thankful for any sound she made, as it indicated she was alive and fighting.

Doc Sam rolled out a metal tank. "She's out like a light, but I won't take the chance she wakes up." He stopped it short of the bed, close to her head. "This little baby will keep her in dreamland while we work. Now, in order to get the arrow out of her, we're going to have to continue the path through the arm."

Jacob grimaced. "*Through* her arm?"

"It's our only choice. It's going to damage her too much to try extracting it. This won't be pleasant, but it's got to be done."

"If it helps her, I don't care," Jacob replied.

Sam inserted an IV from the tank into Jubilee's arm. "This is pretty ugly. Of course, I've seen far worse. Far worse indeed."

Jacob looked at the wall behind him. There were a few old certificates on plaques hanging just above his head. A picture close by showed what looked like Doc Sam, although much younger, with a full head of dark hair and a grin, posing next to a man in a military uniform.

"Looks like you have," Jacob said while staring at the picture.

Doc Sam turned his head. "Oh." He chuckled. "You've caught some of my old memories. Sergeant Dan Sullivan. Good man. Died last year." Jacob then turned to see the doctor's eyes. They looked sad, but then he turned back to Jubilee.

"Dan was the last one. This place is my world now."

"So, you were military?" Jacob asked.

"Yep. Army Ranger medic. Served in the Middle East. When my service was over, I spent the next twenty-five years teaching herbal medicine in other countries. Racked up a lot of miles." He laughed. "I also set up sustainable communities and made sure they had clean sources of water. I'd probably still be out there if my back and legs weren't acting up. It's just a reminder that I'm not young anymore."

So, this man was a genuine doctor. Better yet, he was a very experienced doctor as well. Calm flooded Jacob's tired body. Jubilee was in good hands.

Doc Sam tilted Jubilee on her side. "Alright." He pointed to the back of her arm. "This is where it has to come out. Hold on to her."

Jacob gripped Jubilee as the doctor reached for a scalpel. "Thanks for this. Look, I have money, resources, whatever you want for this, I can give you."

"Let's get this arrow first and then we can talk about paying. Don't be in such a hurry." Doc Sam pointed the scalpel at Jubilee's skin.

Jacob winced as the doctor made the incision. He never had witnessed a surgery, not even a small one. The cutting into the flesh sent tremors down to his toes.

"Easy there, Jacob. She needs you."

Jacob realized his grip was slipping. He tightened his hold as Doc Sam performed his work.

Doc Sam did not rush the operation. Once the incision was made, he took forceps and reached into the cut to grab the arrowhead. He poked very gently. Jacob clenched his jaw. The fact that this scene was happening to his child made it so much worse.

Then the doctor pulled the forceps out, but so slowly that Jacob did not catch the movement until they were almost out. The forceps gripped a small blood-soaked piece of metal.

"So, here's the culprit." Doc Sam frowned as he stared at it. "Some moron was just popping off with these things, huh?" Then he set the forceps on a small metal tray before tending to Jubilee. Now the doctor began cleaning the teenager's wound.

Jacob spotted his face through a small mirror on the doctor's table. It looked a little green. He really had not taken this well, but it all was worth it to help Jubilee.

Doc Sam put the towels he used to clean Jubilee's wound in a disposable plastic bag. "I've got antibiotics on hand. That will help prevent any infections." Then he reached for a set of stitches behind him. "Time to close her up."

In a few minutes, the doctor had sewed up Jubilee's arm wound in front and the incision he had made in back. Throughout the surgical procedure, Jubilee had not made any loud noises. The sedative Doc Sam had given her kept her out for the entire operation.

"She'll need a few days' rest," Doc Sam said as he

gently laid Jubilee on her back. "We'll also have to keep up her antibiotics for the next few days as well."

Jacob let out an anguished breath as if he had been holding it in until he knew his daughter was on the road to recovery. "Thank you," he said with nearly a sob.

Doc Sam stepped up to a sink. "Don't sweat it." He turned the knob. Water flowed through the faucet and washed the doctor's hands. Jacob leaned in close.

"Wait, your water works?"

"*My* water works." Doc Sam chuckled. "It's a handmade pumping system I installed. It runs to my own personal well. It doesn't work off the local water plant." As he wiped his hands, he added, "One of the many things I did to get ready for what was coming."

"Then you knew what was coming?" Jacob asked.

"I'd call it an inkling." Doc Sam dried his hands.

"I've had a sense that the page of history was getting ready to turn. Couldn't say exactly how, but I knew it. My daddy thought the Russians were going to do it, my granddaddy thought it was going to be the Nazis, and my great granddaddy thought a plague was going to get us." He smiled. "I figured maybe Nature would spring a surprise on us."

"A pretty nasty surprise," Jacob said.

"And it's only going to get worse from here." Doc Sam looked Jacob in the eye. "You're an interesting fellow. You're not from Trapp. Where are you from?"

"A homestead near the Blue Ridge Mountains," Jacob replied.

"I see. I figured you were a man who does some work with his hands." He pointed at Jacob's large biceps. "So, that's what all that talk about resources was about? You farm the land?"

"Yes. And we have our own water supply."

"Well, I'll be damned. You weren't kidding." Doc Sam strolled past Jacob.

Jacob followed the doctor toward the door. "I can give you food, water. I even have some medicine..."

"We'll discuss payment soon." Doc Sam emerged into his living room. "I think you'll find my rates are fair." He chuckled. "And a little surprising."

With his daughter successfully treated, Jacob took some time to look around the living room. The doc had installed two glass windows with blinds, one on each side of his front door. With the blind on the right window pulled back, he could see out to a street that ran close to the home.

However, it was sound, not sight that drew Jacob's attention. "What the hell is that?" Jacob asked as he turned toward the glass pane.

Doc Sam looked through the window. "Got somebody in nice clothes arguing with Elliot Christensen. Oh, Elliot's the owner of *Frosters*, hamburger place. It's not far from here."

Jacob looked over Doc Sam's shoulder. Two men were approaching Doc Sam's property. Instantly, he recognized one of the two men. "Son of a bitch. That's Alex Cowell!"

"A friend of yours?" the doc asked.

"Hardly. He's a social worker. He's been harassing me for the past year. He thinks we're depriving our kids of social interaction with others." Jacob's frown deepened. "Along with a bunch of other shit."

"Really? Want me to shoot him for you?" Doc Sam deadpanned.

Jacob almost laughed. "No, I don't think I want that."

The doctor chuckled. "Don't worry. If I wouldn't shoot a lawyer, I don't think I'd treat a social worker any worse. But Elliot's worked up over something. Let's go check it out before it gets bad."

JACOB FOLLOWED Doc Sam out of the house and across the front yard until the doctor stopped at the curb. Jacob turned to the right, in the direction from which Elliot and Cowell were approaching. Elliot, a good half a foot shorter than Cowell, was behind the social worker yelling at him along the way.

Jacob turned to his wife and son, who had remained in Doc Sam's front yard while Jubilee was being treated. He nodded to Domino, who smiled and nodded back. She and Brandon remained where they were, as Jacob had hoped. He didn't want those two in the immediate vicinity of the bickering pair, who by now were so close that Elliot's words rattled Jacob's eardrums.

Cowell, on the other hand, responded with his usual self-assuredness. "If you continue following me, you'll likely spend the night in a jail cell."

"Jail? Me? You arrogant son of a bitch! You're the one who stole from me in the first place!" Elliot erupted, his already reddened round cheeks becoming more crimson from his fury.

"Elliot!" Doc Sam quickened his pace to catch up to the feuding pair. "What's the story?"

"Sam!" Elliot shook his head. "You better watch this guy, or he'll try stealing from you, too. This asshole ate half a plate of chicken and fries that I had prepared for Frances and his kids!"

"I left you twelve dollars," Cowell said as she slowed down. "You could have kept the change. It's more than you deserve after you refused to serve me anything."

"I told you, I closed down today so I could help out my friends and the rest of the people in this town! Do you know what's happened?"

"Yes, I do, and that makes your refusal to serve me even worse. Much of your establishment is outdoors. You allow people to sit on benches and chairs. I saw people eating there besides me, so you have no right to refuse me."

"Those were some of my neighbors coming for help! I guess you didn't see the two ladies sobbing because they're scared of what just happened! I was providing my inventory to them for free, asshole! Because I know it'll go rotten because my fridges are out! And if you were listening, instead of lecturing me on public accommodation laws, you would have understood that!"

"Then why wouldn't you take my money? I told you I would pay. You refused."

Elliot finally calmed down a little, growing a little solemn in the process. "Because money doesn't mean shit anymore."

"It's called the currency of the United States, and until I hear otherwise, we still use it to buy goods and services," Cowell said.

Doc Sam turned to Jacob. "Your social worker friend's head is harder than the hull of an aircraft carrier."

Elliot grinded his teeth a little before continuing. "Look, your money isn't good for anything anymore, not if everything's gone to shit like I think it has. You wanted some food, I'd have accommodated you. You could have lifted some boxes, helped out, something."

Cowell tried to compose himself. "I'm sure whatever is happening is not going to last much longer." He cleared his throat. "But, in the meantime, if arrangements around here have changed, then I'll be happy to go along with whatever you say."

"Good to hear that, sir." Doc Sam slapped Cowell on his right arm. The social worker winced while grimacing in disgust.

"Now, how about you stick around here for a

while? I think you should keep your distance from the town for a while, so you don't run into any more trouble." He winked at Elliot.

"I'm more worried about you, Sam," Elliot said, "You know they're coming."

The doctor nodded. "Yeah. Yeah, I know."

WITH ELLIOT GONE, Jacob turned his attention to his family, quickly explaining that Jubilee would be alright. Jacob and Domino then embraced each other as Domino expressed her great relief for her daughter.

Doc Sam chuckled. "Now then, how about we all go inside?" He glanced at Cowell. "You too."

Cowell straightened out his shirt as much as he could. "Alright."

Jacob frowned. He didn't like the idea of being near Cowell any longer than necessary, but the doctor clearly wanted to keep Cowell away from the town for a while.

Doc Sam pushed open the front door. "And now, my dear Avery family..." He kept the door open while Jacob, Domino and Brandon strolled past. "We can discuss how you will pay me."

CHAPTER SEVEN

JACOB KEPT an eye on his family's reactions as they stepped into the doctor's home. Brandon was the most wide-eyed and attentive, perhaps the result of a child's natural curiosity. Domino's smile grew as she gazed around the room, likely reinforcing whatever she had been thinking of Doc Sam as she waited outside.

As for Alex Cowell, the social worker was trying to keep his dignity as he entered the house. He maintained that same serene if mildly disdainful gaze he possessed whenever he strolled around Jacob's property.

"This place is neat!" Brandon peered into the room where Doc Sam operated on Jubilee. "It's like a lab. A mad scientist's lab!"

Jacob cringed a bit, as he didn't know if their benefactor would take offense. Domino tried to stifle a laugh and mostly failed.

Doc Sam, however, let out a roaring laugh. "Is that right? A mad scientist, huh?" The doctor then advanced quickly on Brandon. "Well, you're a brave boy to come walking into my lair, aren't you?" He pointed to a closet in the living room. "In fact, you better not open that door!"

"Why not?" Brandon asked, still smiling as if he sensed the doctor was ribbing him.

"That's where I keep all the bodies I experiment on. In fact, they are known to..." Doc Sam leaned a little closer. "...escape during the night."

"Cool!" Brandon said.

As Brandon and Doc Sam chatted, Cowell had slipped past the pair so he could enter the doctor's treatment room and look at the certificates on the walls. "M.D.," he said quietly, but loud enough for Jacob to hear.

Doc Sam turned his head. "Checking my credentials, are you? I guess old habits die hard with you. I hear you've been somewhat of a pain in the sides of my guests."

"They tell only one side of the story," Cowell said, not averting his eyes from the certificates. "I just do my job. That involves making sure the welfare of children like Jubilee here..." He looked back at the sleeping Jubilee. "...is secure."

Jacob's blood started to boil as Doc Sam walked into the room and took Cowell by the arm. "Well, it's secure enough here, thank you. Now how about you step out of here and let the girl rest?"

Cowell allowed Doc Sam to usher him out of the room until he broke free and walked past the Averys. Then he stopped near the living room's far window.

"Now." Doc Sam clapped his hands softly. "About payment. As you likely know, paper currency isn't of any value any more unless you need to burn it for warmth. In any case, my policy is simple. Everything I used to heal your child, I receive it back. You have the responsibility. Every resource I used to treat Jubilee is due back to me in payment."

Domino and Jacob exchanged glances. Jacob figured Domino was thinking the same thing. Where would they find the supplies Doc Sam wanted? Jacob thought back to Jubilee's surgery. If Doc Sam wanted fresh scalpels, Jacob had those at the homestead. He had bulked up on medical supplies in anticipation of a disaster. But would Doc Sam allow them to travel that far to retrieve them? Without the use of an automobile, it would be days before they could make it back here.

I'm sure he would be reasonable, Jacob thought. *If he wants us to bring him these supplies, he has to know it won't be lightning quick*.

"That sounds fair," Jacob said. "Do you have a list of what you need?"

Doc Sam yawned. "Not now. I'll do that later."

"And do you know where we can find these supplies?" Domino asked.

Sam smiled. "Don't worry. I won't make this hard on you. But first..." He tapped his stomach. "I'm starving and I'm sure you all could use a good meal. Once we've filled our bellies, I'll give you the lowdown on what you need."

SAM PEELED the foil off the smoking leg of lamb. "Now that, my dear family, is going to taste like heaven." He loudly inhaled the wisps of steam rising from the meat. "Yessiree."

In the dining room, Jacob inhaled the wafting scent of the lamb. He absolutely agreed with Doc Sam. Even though Jacob and Domino frequently cooked meat for the family and knew how good freshly cooked meat smelled, this lamb smelled more delicious than their past efforts.

With all the craziness in the world, I guess we know how to appreciate everything that we can enjoy, Jacob thought.

With gloved hands, Doc Sam carried the metal pan that held the lamb toward the dinner table. The Averys plus Cowell waited, though Cowell sat on the far end, isolated from everyone else.

After discarding the gloves, Sam reached for a long fork and knife. "Lady gets first cut." He turned slightly at Jacob, who was seated to his left. "If you know what's good for you, right?"

Jacob chuckled. "Yeah, I guess so."

Domino winked at her husband as she raised her plate. Sam playfully dropped the slice onto it.

"Now, for the boy." Doc Sam carved a second piece. "How old are you, son?"

"Nine," said Brandon, seated next to Domino.

"Ah, getting old enough to be a lady killer." Sam dropped a slice on Brandon's plate. "I hope your folks taught you proper manners."

Jacob cleared his throat. "I have good kids."

"I bet you do." Doc Sam turned his attention to Jacob's slice of meat.

Jacob eyed the lamb before him. "Do I have to replace the lamb, too?"

"Sure, you feel like finding a ram and an ewe, treat them to dinner, get them in the sack, have them give birth and raise the new lamb for me?"

Jacob, his eyes widened, froze as Doc Sam passed the slice to his plate.

The doctor then shook his head, followed by a hearty laugh. Jacob breathed a sigh of relief. The doctor was just kidding. Sometimes it was hard to tell, though.

"And as for you, sir." Doc Sam narrowed his eyes at Cowell. "I trust you are not a vegetarian."

Cowell sat up. "No. I-I would appreciate some dinner. Thanks."

THE GROUP ATE their lamb along with roasted potatoes. The Averys did not realize how starved they all were. In all the chaos of the day, they had not even eaten lunch. They had expended so much energy getting here that they needed every morsel of food to replenish themselves.

"So, you all, the Avery family." Sam pointed his fork to the Averys close by him. "I presume you have a home to get home to." He chuckled.

"It's not far. It's a homestead out in the country," Jacob said.

"So, in other words, there's nobody's around you. Let's say, you don't live with neighbors just a few steps down the walkway," Doc Sam said.

"No." Jacob cast a glance at Domino. "It's like our little personal world. We have our crops, our own sources of energy, our own well."

"And weapons?" Doc Sam asked.

Jacob wiped his mouth. "Yeah. Yeah, we have our own weapons, too."

Now Cowell spoke up for the first time since accepting Sam's dinner. "Preppers."

"Excuse me?" Sam leaned in.

"Preppers. People who believe society is headed for a catastrophe. They prepare to live without dependency on outside help. Canning food, digging your own water, stocking up on clothes and medicine. And, of course, there's weapons." Cowell cast an eye on Jacob. "I'm sure you are well stocked."

Jacob wiped his mouth uneasily. "I wouldn't call myself a prepper. That's not why I moved out there with Domino."

"Well then, why did you?" Doc Sam asked.

Jacob looked down at his plate. He always had tried to minimize talk of his past around Cowell as much as possible, but with society effectively flat on its back, Jacob did not have to worry much about Cowell any longer. "I used to live in a pretty rough neighborhood up near D.C. The valley near the Blue Ridge Mountains was a place we could get away. Over time, as I learned how to live off the land, I explored ways to keep us self-sufficient. It was just natural. The more we built our own life, the more we wanted to keep it that way."

Doc Sam nodded. "Well, I suppose whether you intended to or not, you became preppers. There's no shame in that."

Brandon glared at Cowell. "Is that why you don't like my family? Because you don't like preppers?"

Cowell coughed. He quickly wiped his lips before replying. "I don't dislike your family. My problem is that people with the mentality that the world is going to collapse around them are prone to dangerous lifestyle choices. They delve into their own paranoia so deeply that they injure those they claim to love, deprive them, and in some cases abuse them. And if they become truly fanatical in their beliefs, they may end the lives of those around them."

Jacob's right hand tightened as Cowell spoke, fueled by Jacob's growing resentment of this man and his judgmental attitude. He might have snapped if Doc Sam hadn't intervened.

"There are those out there with many screws

loose, that is true. But it sounds as though you paint some people with too broad a brush, Mister Social Worker. Fanaticism knows no particular ideology." The doctor ate a small piece of lamb before continuing. "In any case, I think there was a certain logic in prepping. You never know what can fall on your head. God knows a lot of people didn't."

"I don't believe this," Cowell said. "There's no way in hell the federal government didn't prepare for whatever this event was. Even if the whole country is shut down, and I hardly buy that, there are contingencies. There have to be."

"You want to bet your pasty white ass on that?" Doc Sam asked.

Domino rolled her eyes. Doc Sam quickly turned to her and said, "Sorry. Kids arc present." Then he winked at Brandon before continuing. "Anyway, my good social worker, I'm sure the geniuses in Washington probably did make some preparations. The problem is that it's nothing better than a drop of spit in an empty bucket when you need to fill up the damn thing. Ever watch C-SPAN? Sure, they debated all kinds of packages and funding and what not, and it never got anywhere." Sam shrugged. "Now, it's too late."

"Even if things are really that bad, they can mobilize the army. They can keep the country together while they fix things," Cowell said.

"And how are they going to mobilize the army? They can't call them up on the phone. How many radios you think they got working? Maybe they'll use smoke signals?"

Cowell rolled his eyes. "I refuse to believe Washington can be caught this flat-footed!"

"Well, believe it. You have no choice but to assume the worst. Without communication, the government's bound to disintegrate as everyone tries figuring out how to save their own skins. Because the D.C. area is filled with more than a million people who are very confused, scared, and soon to be desperate. And desperate people do pretty horrific things."

"We're not uncivilized people. If we get the message from the President to stay indoors, wait, follow instructions..."

"My God, you are stupid as hell!" Doc Sam threw his head back and laughed.

Cowell didn't quite raise himself fully out of his seat, but he did rise high enough to overshadow his plate. "Now that is uncalled for!"

"I'd say it's very much called for. I'm trying to tear down those rose-colored illusions of yours. Life as you know it is over. No help is coming. As of today, we all provide for ourselves. And I mean everything, especially the food you eat and the water you drink. You can't go to the supermarket to buy them. If you want them, you have to barter from someone who does have them or else get the water and food yourself."

Cowell opened his mouth, but then stopped as if he recognized his current line of arguing wasn't getting anywhere. So, he settled back down and resumed his meal.

However, the subject matter of the conversation still weighed heavily on Jacob's mind. Now that Jubilee had been treated for her wounds, he had time to consider the implications of the future, and how different—and scary—it would be.

"Doctor," Jacob said, "what can we expect? I've studied EMPs, but I don't understand the full impact."

Doc Sam finished off his last bite of lamb. "Well, it's going to be terrible. In fact, I'd say the word hasn't been invented to describe what's going to happen. Over a million people already have died today. The pulse has taken out airport electronics. Anything in the air came crashing down to Earth. Add in cars, trains, that's more crashes, so that's more dead. But from here on out, it just goes from worse to worse."

The doctor cleared his throat. "No electricity means no way to refrigerate food or to send it around the country. Millions of people alone are going to starve to death. EMPs also knock out water sanitation plants. So, you never know what you're drinking. It could have bacteria, pollutants. Point is, bad water's going to kill off millions, too. And, of course, no electricity means no working hospitals or clinics. So, our advanced medical tech just hit the crapper. So that kills off millions more who can't get treated."

Domino swallowed a piece of lamb very slowly

before asking her question. "How far is this going to go?"

"The estimate is perhaps 90 percent of the American population's going under," Sam said, without hesitation.

"My God." Domino let her fork rest on her plate.

A silence swept over them. No one knew what to say, leaving it up to Sam to jump back in.

"Like I said, I'm here to tear down rose-colored illusions. There's no easy way to get the power grid back up. One transformer weighs several tons. You shut off the vehicles too, and there's no way to transport a new transformer anywhere. It'll take years to get the grid back up, or any grid for that matter." Sam stirred the last of his potatoes.

Cowell pressed his napkin against his face, which now looked green.

CHAPTER EIGHT

JACOB AND DOC Sam sat on the back porch as the doctor wrote down a list of the items he wanted. Everything down to the sutures was on it. A glass of bourbon rested next to Doc Sam.

"So, how's your friend doing?" Doc Sam asked, "The social worker? I think I overheard him puking outside."

"I don't think it was your food," Jacob said.

"Better not be." Doc Sam chuckled. "I guess I can't blame him. I'm sure he didn't expect to wake up this morning and know that he would lose just about everything." He scratched his chin. "Even if his lot in life was going after you."

"It's alright. I'd rather be dealing with him than have all this happen."

Doc Sam pointed to the items on the list. "Here you go. Sutures, antibiotics, the whole shooting match. I know some of this isn't going to be easy."

"It's fine. You helped my daughter. There's no way I can say no." Jacob looked back at the house. "I should think about looking for a hotel for my family."

"Good luck. The local hotels are going to be full, assuming their workers haven't fled or anything," Doc Sam said. "Your family can stay here."

"Do you need to add anything to the list, for the room and board?" Jacob handed the list back to him.

"No, no. I do not charge extra for board. The only thing I ask is that you get on that list quickly." Doc Sam gazed at the land beyond his house.

"There's a wave coming. People are going to need help, and it's not like I can buy more supplies from a dealer. I don't know what would happen if I ran out of medicine and supplies." Doc Sam turned to his glass of bourbon. "They might string me up!" He then burst out laughing.

Jacob nearly laughed, but he found it hard to find humor in their current situation. He had not fully processed what was going on and he doubted he would for a long while.

His hand brushed against his belt. He fingered the cell phone in the holster. "I was about to take a picture of the list." Now he could laugh, if only because of the absurdity of this situation. "In case I lost it." He pulled out the phone and waved its blank screen around. "I had to remind myself that the phone doesn't work anymore."

Doc Sam smiled. "You're going to be like that for a while. Habits are going to die hard. For a while you're going to keep reaching for things that just don't work anymore. Phones, television remotes, computers..." He sighed. "We all got too hooked on that kind of stuff. Now we're paying the price." His eyes met Jacob's. "Why'd you move out into the country? I know your social worker buddy said a lot of stuff. What do you have to say about it?"

Jacob tucked his phone away. "I was born in Alexandria. My father wasn't married to my mother. He popped in a few times every now and then. When I was about nine, he stopped completely. Heard he ended up in jail somewhere in South Carolina. That's the last I ever heard." He rested his chin on his knuckle. "I was surrounded by tough guys. For a while I wanted to be like them. But I saw pretty quickly that they were trouble, big trouble."

Doc Sam took a swig of bourbon while Jacob continued. "They didn't like me trying to get out of 'the life.' They saw me as an easy mark. Then I tried fighting back. I got in a few good hits, but the funny thing about being outnumbered is that you're, well, outnumbered." Jacob rubbed his face above his right eyelid. "Won't forget the hit I took here." Jacob draped his hands on his knees. "But, if it wasn't for all that, I wouldn't have met Domino."

"She was one of the bad girls?" Doc Sam asked.

"Rebellious is more like it. She actually came from money. She lived in Alexandria. Her parents were rich. Like a lot of people in that town, they dealt with the federal government. They went to parties, hung out with celebrities, lobbyists, went on foreign trips, all of which Domino hated. For a while she even hated her own name because the kids kept asking her if she worked at Domino's Pizza."

"They sound like kooky folks," Doc Sam said.

"I think so," Jacob replied. "Well, they didn't care for her rebelling and she didn't care for their lifestyle. A rift grew between them pretty quickly. She dyed her hair, became a platinum blonde, and did her best to keep her distance from them. For a while she ran with the same crowd who took their shots at me, but she quickly realized she didn't want to be with them, and that I was different. We fell for each other pretty hard our junior year in high school."

"So, what led you two to come out to the country?" Doc Sam asked.

"I didn't want my kids to grow up in the same hell I did," Jacob said.

"When I was little, I'd see those fairy tale movies. They'd always be in a forest somewhere and I always thought of them as magical places. Of course, today I know you have to work hard to live in the forest." He chuckled. "There's no magic out here. Well, maybe there is. The last fifteen years have been the best. The best for both of us."

Doc Sam finished off his glass. "Sounds like you ended up in a fairy tale after all. You got a happily ever after." He set his glass down. "At least so far."

Jacob nodded. "So far."

JACOB LOOKED THROUGH THE DOOR. Jubilee was sleeping on the bed inside the small room. Domino, on her knees, was leaning close to her daughter.

As Jacob approached, Domino said, "I wiped her face. She doesn't feel as warm. I think she's doing better."

"Doc Sam thinks she should wake up soon, probably as early as tomorrow," Jacob said.

"I wish I could sleep next to her," Domino said.

"Yeah. But the doc wants her to rest alone until her wound has had some time to heal. We don't know what situation her immune system is in," Jacob said.

"Right." Domino sighed. "Terrible thing to hear that you can't be too close to your own baby."

She turned around. Jacob reached down. Domino took his hand and allowed him to lift her up. "You know," Jacob said quietly, "our kids have had a good life away from the city. But it's not like our world was a perfect shield. She was hit by an arrow. You wouldn't see those in the suburbs."

"Maybe not, but you might see a bullet instead." Domino flicked loose hair out of Jacob's face. "Life's never perfect. There's going to be risks no matter where you go."

A shadow moved along the wall. Jacob turned to the right. Cowell was hovering in the living room beyond the door, looking uneasy, as if he did not know what to do next. Doc Sam had been tending to some end of the day tasks such as making sure the home was locked up for the evening.

As it so happened, Doc Sam returned to the living room from a side door. Cowell, his arms folded, said to him, "I thank you for your hospitality."

"Well, you're very welcome," Doc Sam replied.

Cowell looked to the front door. "I suppose there is a hotel in this town?"

"There is that small place, Ben's Motel, on the other side of Trapp, but God knows what shape it is now. Personally, I wouldn't go for it. I don't know if Ben is taking in new guests with what's going on now, and besides, hotels might be dangerous places right now. You never know if somebody decides to, well, *carpe diem*. You might end up on the wrong end of that."

Cowell scowled. "I'd be attacked by some hoodlum or robber?"

"This world is going to make robbers out of a lot of people." Doc Sam glanced at the couch by the wall. "My suggestion? Bunk out on there for the night. I'm not going to turn you loose to the wolves."

"You would let me stay?" Cowell asked.

"Sure. Not forever, of course. I intend to give you the boot as soon as it's feasible."

Cowell frowned. "Thanks."

"That's not a jab at you, Mister Social Worker," Doc Sam said as Cowell walked to the sofa. "This place may become too busy for anyone to rest comfortably. You won't be the last people to show up looking for help."

Cowell sat down. "You sound a little worried about that."

Doc Sam nodded. "Some of those people aren't going to be as neighborly as the Averys or yourself. You might want to get away from here soon if you can."

Blood.

It laid a long trail across the ground leading from the shadow of his homestead. Jacob tracked it. He hoped it wasn't human. If it was human, he feared who the blood belonged to.

I'm dreaming.

Jacob quickened his pace, but not so quickly that he lost the trail. He observed how the blood coated small leaves and blades of grass. He almost could tell the blood was familiar, although it shouldn't be possible. Blood was blood. How could he tell who it belonged to?

Perhaps because he was afraid of who it belonged to.

I'm dreaming.

Jacob jogged past his rows of crops. He did not look up at the horizon. He wanted to know where the hell this trail of blood led. Nothing else mattered to him.

I'm dreaming...aren't I?

He was now beyond his crops. His footsteps took him toward the open area of his land where his children loved to play. He was rapidly closing the gap between himself and the pond.

Please God, let me be dreaming.

The trail of blood led behind a tall patch of cattails. Jacob scurried to the banks of the pond. Once there, he understood what he had been tracking all along.

Jubilee lay on the ground, the arrowhead embedded in her arm. Blood trickled down her arm, and she breathed heavily. The teen looked up at the skies with wide but placid eyes.

What's she looking at?

The pond's water reflected the skies above, but instead of a serene blue heaven, white clouds, or even a stormy sky, the waters displayed a sky on fire. Jacob trembled. Was all of that right above him?

He didn't want to look up. But he had to. A compulsion within his body demanded it.

Upon looking up, Jacob beheld the terrible sight above. He thought for a moment he saw God himself in the sky. A human-like figure had taken shape from a blue cloud. But then Jacob saw a second shape forming from a green cloud close by. Were there two gods up there? Or angels? Or demons?

Maybe this is the end of the world, Jacob thought. Perhaps the destruction of the world's electricity and electronics was ordained from Heaven itself. Jacob was not a particularly religious man, but he was at least familiar with the broad strokes of the Bible, including the parts about angels pouring out God's wrath upon the world.

However, these celestial forms seemed to be looking down on him. An added chill ran down Jacob's back. Why were they looking at him? Were they judging him for something? Perhaps they looked at him as just a part of humanity as a whole and regarded him as no less guilty than the others.

"I know."

Jacob turned his head. His daughter was pointing to the strange entities above.

"We'll never make it," she finished.

The weight of the previous day seemed finally to hit home. His world had changed. The weight of the burden he now had to bear in making sure his family was safe from the horrors emerging around him felt crushing.

Then he woke up.

Clutching the white sheet, Jacob looked around the guest room where he and his wife were sleeping. Jubilee slept soundlessly in a bed near the wall opposite them while Brandon slumbered in another room next door. The room was quiet. There was no sound of air conditioning. Soft chirping penetrated through the glass of the small window.

He patted his white undershirt. Sweat had soaked into it. Jacob rarely had slept without an air conditioner's soft breeze blowing on him, and it was fairly warm outside, even with the sun down. However, Jacob suspected the wild dream he just had experienced explained his sweat a lot better.

He rolled onto his side, facing his sleeping wife, who reclined on her side. Sweat dripped down her face. He wondered if the lack of air conditioning was taxing her a little, but as he watched her face contort, Jacob guessed that she might be dreaming too, and not having good ones.

But then her eyes opened. Jacob froze in place, to wait for her to drop back to sleep if she could. Instead she awoke fully.

"Hey," Jacob said, "bad dreams?"

"Yeah," she replied, "you?"

"Yeah. Bad, bizarre, troubling." Jacob clutched the sheet tighter. "I guess with everything that's happened, I should be glad my dreams aren't worse than they are."

Domino smiled sadly. "I used to be able to chase away your bad dreams. Remember that night, in that hotel room in Alexandria?"

Jacob smiled. "Well, you did a good job of chasing away bad dreams. Of course, that was also the first time we..."

"Had sex for the first time?" Domino asked.

Jacob chuckled. "I was going to say, 'made love.'"

"My God, you are getting old. You're becoming too classy," Domino said with a soft laugh.

"Maybe." Jacob chuckled some more.

"Anyway, I don't know what my dreams mean. I

guess I'm afraid that I won't be able to..." He pointed to the ceiling. "...handle all of this. I've read about what can happen when society goes into the shitter, but it is scary to see it all happen in front of you. I mean, if it was just me, or even just the two of us, I wouldn't be this way, but with the kids, I worry about them." He sighed. "I suppose you don't want to hear me say that. It sounds better if I have it all together, doesn't it?"

"I'd be surprised if you weren't scared," Domino said, "but you're doing fine. You got Jubilee help even in the midst of this madness."

"With your help," Jacob quickly added.

"Yes, thank you, thank you." Domino nodded her head twice as if to imitate a person bowing on stage.

"I just wish I didn't have to leave you," Jacob said.

"We'll be fine. Trust me. I can handle Alex Cowell," Domino said.

Jacob laughed. "Well, I'm not worried about Cowell. Not completely, anyway. You know what I mean."

"Right. This seems like a good town, good people. I don't think we're in any immediate danger." Domino looked down at the bed. "And you know that I can take care of myself."

"I do."

Jacob thought about the early years when he knew Domino. He knew that Domino was tough. Even so, he dreaded the idea that Domino would have to defend herself again. He had thought that their homestead, situated close to rural communities, would have been far enough away from seedy elements to avoid violent confrontations.

Sadly, the arrow in Jubilee's arm dispelled much of that notion. It only would get worse from here.

"Jay, try to get some sleep." Domino ran a hand through Jacob's hair. "You need all your strength tomorrow."

"I'll try." Jacob rolled onto his back. It would not be easy. Perhaps his wife would be able to chase away his bad dreams once again.

CHAPTER NINE

JACOB MANAGED a few hours of sleep, but his eyes fluttered open before the sun rose. It was just as well, for Doc Sam approached quietly through the doorway. He cast a glance at Jubilee. The doctor perhaps did not want to wake up her or Domino, who still was sleeping. Jacob silently thanked him for showing caution.

"It's almost five a.m.," Doc Sam said, "still have some clocks that work. Join me in the kitchen. Leave the lady be. It's time we plan your trip."

Jacob exhaled softly. "Alright."

DOC SAM FLATTENED the map on the kitchen table. "Now, ordinarily this wouldn't be a big deal. I order my supplies from a dealer in Pleasantville. But, of course, phones and email went into the crapper yesterday, so calling ahead to arrange an order is out of the question." He looked up, his eyes meeting Jacob's. "Without communication, you won't know what to expect."

"I've been to Pleasantville. The interstate runs right through it. It's one of the main arteries into the D.C. metro area. In fact, there's an airport not far from there." Jacob bit his lower lip. "Doc, there's no way I can go any farther than Pleasantville. Hell, even Pleasantville itself might be clogged with people. There's going to be a whole stream just pouring out of there."

"A stream of desperate people. I agree. I don't want to put you in unnecessary danger." The doctor traced a path downward along the interstate south of Pleasantville. "There are some towns along the way, smaller places, perhaps locales that won't be as dangerous. Middleburg, now there's somewhere you can try. Doctor Nguyen lives there. He's helped me out on occasion. In fact, he might even have the antibiotics I used on your daughter. Yes, yes, I recommend you try him first."

Doc Sam scrambled to fish out a pad and pen from the counter. "Let me write down the address." After scribbling the information and tearing the page from the pad, he added, "Don't worry about paying him for the supplies. I'll give you some proof that you know me." He pushed the paper into Jacob's open hand. "He and I go back some years. In fact, he accompanied me into some overseas trips to Vietnam and Burma to help some of the communities there."

Doc Sam sighed. Jacob asked, "It sounds like the trip didn't go well."

"He was quite happy to return home, let's put it that way. I only hope he's able to handle this disaster. In his younger years, I'd have no doubt." Doc Sam returned to the map. "It's on Madison Drive. Here." He pointed to a street not far from the interstate. "You'll take your own map with you."

"Don't worry. I have one in my get home bag," Jacob said.

"Your what?"

"My get home bag is what I packed to sustain me if I wound up away from home without a car or anyway to get home quickly."

Doc Sam laughed. "My God, you think of so much. I can't believe you never intended to be a prepper."

"I guess it's now in my blood. I've learned so much since I began my life on my farm. If I have to, I can make fire, sanitize water, build a shelter." Jacob eyed the interstate that ran up the left half of the paper map, envisioning the journey to come. It excited and frightened him all at once.

He was so deep in thought he did not hear the footsteps of Alex Cowell or see the shadow that crossed his arm until the social worker had made it past him and was closing in on the refrigerator. Jacob raised his head. Cowell looked pretty rough. His once stern eyes now turned down to the floor, his strait gait was crooked, and his shirttail hung out of the pants.

"The fridge doesn't work," Jacob said as Cowell reached for the handle.

Cowell's hand dropped down. "Damn. I forgot." He turned away without looking at Jacob or Doc Sam.

"You look like you had a rough night, sailor," Doc Sam said.

"I tried, but it was hard to sleep." Cowell shuffled along the counter. He seemed finally to bear the weight of the terrible revelation that the world around him had gone to hell. "Do you have something to drink? I need something, anything."

"Water will do in a pinch." Doc Sam turned to Jacob. "Pour some for him if you would."

"Sure."

Jacob found a paper cup and walked up to Doc Sam's small water cooler. He pushed down on the button and waited for the cup to fill with water. Although the electricity was gone, and the cooler no longer could chill its water, it still was a handy way to quickly find some water around here.

Cowell took the cup and drank, but he expressed no thanks beyond a single, curt nod. Jacob decided any further words were not forthcoming, so he turned back to the map.

"A get home bag," Cowell suddenly spoke up.

Jacob craned his head back to Cowell. "What?"

"How do you think of things like that?" Cowell asked, "It seems ridiculous."

"Not so ridiculous now, don't you think?" Doc Sam spoke up.

"Sure, now, but earlier, when everything was normal." Cowell took a big swig before continuing. "Why the hell did I not hear about this?" Anger rose in his voice. "Why didn't anyone talk about this?"

"I guess you wouldn't hear about it unless you knew where to look," Jacob said.

"So, the only place we'd learn about this kind of stuff, about get home bags and building campfires and whatever other shit you have to know, oh, it's not in schools, not at work, not at government meetings. No, it's just floating on the fringes of the Net. Only they know about all of this!"

It was hard for Jacob not to sympathize with Cowell. Like so many other people just living their lives, they wouldn't have been exposed to the kind of survival skills that Jacob had learned. It didn't seem necessary. They didn't live in a wilderness. Their world was a paragon of advanced technology and convenience. Even though EMP awareness had spiked in recent years, a lot of people never dreamed their modern lifestyle could be ripped away from them.

Cowell placed the empty paper cup on the counter. "I should let you get back to your..." He spun his finger. "Your..." He didn't finish the sentence, instead began walking back through the door.

JACOB CHECKED the contents of his get home bag once again. It was well stocked with everything he would need. *Still, maybe I should unzip this small compartment one more time...*

He was stalling. He needed to admit he was well packed and move on. The sooner he tended to his family, the sooner he could leave and retrieve what Doc Sam wanted.

You could carry Jubilee out of here. If you split from the house at the right moment, while Doc Sam is busy, you could escape scot free and wouldn't have to worry about going to Middleburg or anywhere you think is too dangerous.

A tempting thought. But one, ultimately, he wouldn't entertain. That would make him no better than the thugs he used to live around. He wanted to be better than they were.

He turned from his bed to his sleeping daughter. Her cheeks showed some more color. She was recovering, no question about it. Jacob even dreaded it a little. If she woke up this morning, he would have to explain that he had to leave. Would she insist he stay? Would she be so disoriented that she couldn't bear to have him leave so soon?

I promise I'll be back as soon as I can, Jacob said silently.

With his bag in hand, Jacob stepped through the door into the living room. Domino, seated on the couch with Brandon, was talking to her son.

"But Mom, I can help Dad out!" Brandon was protesting.

"Sweetie, I'm sure you can be a big help, but your dad can make this trip quicker if he's by himself. Besides, it's dangerous out there," Domino said.

Brandon sank back into the couch. "What if he meets a cyborg? I can hack into his programming and make him do our bidding."

"Not a bad idea." Jacob leaned over his son. "And I can't think of anyone better for the job if I run into any cyborgs out there. But your mom's right. This needs to go quickly, and if no one else is with me, I can make it in and out of Middleburg that much easier. Besides, I need you to watch over your sister. What if the cyborgs come for her instead of me?"

"There you go," Domino added.

"Cyborgs wouldn't come for her." Brandon grinned. "The aliens would because she's their long lost princess."

Domino rubbed Brandon's head. "Oh, you."

Jacob leaned lower over Brandon. "Besides, I really do want you to look after Jubilee, especially with Cowell hanging around. He's a little upset about what's going on. I don't think he'll be trouble, but it's best to keep a few eyes around."

Brandon nodded. "Okay."

Jacob hugged his son. "Good."

After parting from Brandon, Jacob stood up and locked eyes with his wife. "I know you can handle yourself, but I still hate leaving you."

Domino nodded. "I know." She hugged him. "We'll be waiting for you when you get back."

JACOB FELT the two straps that ran over his shoulders. His get home bag rested firmly on his back. A soft wind blew through his hair. Domino and Brandon stood to his left with Doc Sam to his right. They were in front of Doc Sam's home, with Cowell milling about near the cacti. Jacob eyed the road running past the doctor's property. The ground sloped up a hill to the left. He could not see beyond it.

"There but the grace of God go you," Doc Sam said, "I'll do whatever it takes to keep your family safe and sound until you return."

Jacob offered his hand. "Thanks, for everything." Doc Sam shook it.

After shaking the doctor's hand, Jacob glanced at Cowell. The man straightened up, putting his hands in his pockets. Just when Jacob thought Cowell would not say anything, Cowell piped up. "Watch yourself out there."

Jacob nodded before turning back to the road. Now he was ready to go.

Doc Sam didn't say anything while Domino and Brandon watched Jacob hike out on the road and eventually out of sight. Jacob's departure confirmed the doctor's curiosity about the man. Jacob Avery was a decent, honorable and courageous individual. He and his family were willing to do all they could to repay him.

The truth of the matter was that Doc Sam was a lot more flexible in his transaction policy than he led on. He was both heartened and saddened to meet the Averys—heartened that Jacob was adept in survival skills, but saddened because he knew these people would be the few exceptions. Most of the people Doc Sam would meet in the coming days would not be that way. They would be scared, desperate people torn out of lives of comfort and predictability. Some would not even be able to handle the kind of journey that Jacob was about to undertake. Sending such people out to replenish his supplies would be a death sentence.

The sound of Cowell's footsteps interrupted his deep thoughts. "Now that Mister Avery has left, I presume we'll be discussing..."

"Yes, yes." Doc Sam smiled crookedly. "The last few steps before I send you on your way. I'm sure you won't want to waste any time, but I do have some issues to take care of with the Avery family."

Cowell nodded. "I'll be waiting inside."

The doctor waited for Cowell to return to the abode. Now it was time to proceed with his business with the Averys. Turning to them, he said, "Okay. While we're waiting for Jacob to return, I think it's time I showed you my bunker."

Domino and Brandon turned around. "Bunker?" Domino asked.

CHAPTER TEN

DOC SAM PUSHED OPEN the garage door. "A little place to seek refuge when times go bad. This garage actually predates my house by a good couple of years. The house that actually was built here, I tore that down." He laughed. "It didn't fit my personality."

Compared to the doctor's home, the garage was far more normal. The left side was taken up by a workbench covered with work tools and parts. Shelves and hooks on the wall held even more. A pale green pickup took up much of the center. The pickup bed was covered with a tarp, and from the way it bubbled up in spots, it obviously still was loaded with cargo.

However, Doc Sam didn't linger around his vehicle. Instead, he walked up to a large old shelving unit. Compared to the other shelves, this set of metal shelves was not well occupied. They were littered only by a few old cardboard boxes.

The doc stopped by the shelves. “Whoops! Now, where did I put that bunker, anyway? Damn, I keep misplacing that thing.” He groped the shelves as if he was a blind man.

“Wait, wait, oh hell, I remember it.” Abruptly, he grabbed onto a shelf post and shifted the shelves outward like an opening door.

Domino and Brandon quickly backed up, nearly hitting the truck behind them.

“Well, appearances sure are deceiving, aren’t they?” Doc Sam then tore off the tape binding one of the boxes. With a flip of the lid, Doc Sam revealed the box was packed with Styrofoam.

“To the naked eye, you’d think these things were pretty heavy, wouldn’t you say? Not so much if you actually open them up.” With a wink, he closed the box back up.

“So, this is all a trick!” Brandon said.

“You betcha.” With the shelf out of the way, Doc Sam reached for the exposed wall.

“Little things like that discourage people from thinking there might be something here.” He ran his finger along a crack in the drywall.

“Thank God I never put any spackle here.” The doc jabbed his finger into the crack and pulled open a small section of the wall like a door, enough to reach inside. Doc Sam had exposed a metal handle. “If I did, I wouldn’t be able to open this door.”

Doc Sam pulled on the handle.

A whole portion of the wall opened up. This part

of the wall was actually a hidden door. "And that, my dear Avery family, is what we call magic."

Brandon's eyes widened. "Cool!"

Doc Sam had exposed a small corridor that descended into the ground. The doc put his foot on the first of the steps that led downward. "Follow me."

Brandon and Domino trailed the doc down the steps until the corridor terminated at a closed door. "That door back there actually has a handle in the back. You can pull it closed behind you. It also slides the shelf back in place." Doc Sam grasped the knob. "Now, here we are." With a turn of the knob, Doc Sam opened up his underground bunker.

The room was clean, very clean. Even the air smelled good. In addition to the bunker's main room, there were also a few doors. Doc Sam, perhaps sensing their curiosity, walked up to one of the doors and opened it, revealing a closet well stocked with bottled water, canned food, and other small containers.

"Too bad I didn't get to show Jacob this before he left." He picked up one of the cans. "Tell me, lady, what do you think? Jacob says you can your food. Did I do a good job?"

Domino took the jar from Doc Sam. "It looks perfect." With a light laugh, she turned the jar upside down. The meat and potatoes inside were so tightly packed that nothing inside shifted.

"Now, I don't advertise that I have this bounty. It's not because I don't want to help people out, but

I'm afraid some discretion's going to be warranted. If the wrong people found out about this place..." Not finishing the sentence, Doc Sam walked over to the next door and opened it. This time he exposed a whole armory.

"Whoa." Brandon's mouth dropped open.

Doc Sam looked up at the gun rack against the left side of the wall. "Prepared for peace or war." He turned to the two Averys. "Hopefully, it won't get too bad. But if it does, this is where you need to run to."

Domino bit her lip. "We will."

Doc Sam gently took the jar from Domino. "Now that you know where this place is, I think we should get back to your daughter. I don't want her to wake up without you nearby, or worse, maybe she wakes up and runs into that social worker of yours."

JACOB AVERY WAS ALONE.

It was a strange feeling. He was walking on this road that took him toward Middleburg, with no traveling companions, nobody to talk to, nobody even to look at as he journeyed. True, he was mostly alone when he was trying to get back to his family on the highway yesterday, but he wasn't going on an extended trip without them. He felt sure he would run into his wife and children within the coming hours.

The silence only reinforced his solitude. No automobiles drove past him on this road. Jacob stuck to the road's shoulder, an instinctual reaction to the possibility that a car would hit him if he walked in the dead center of one of the lanes. But none came. The EMP would have knocked out all automobiles with electronics. Sure, older vehicles would have survived the pulse, but the chances of running into one of them would be slim.

Also, if somebody still had a working car, that person would want to get away from large population areas as soon as possible. Jacob shivered at the thought. The unfortunate bastard likely would get mobbed and killed for his vehicle.

Hell, people are going to rob and kill for the smallest morsels, Jacob thought.

He kept walking. Soon he realized something was wrong. He ought to have reached the turnoff onto State Road 219 by now. Why was it taking so long?

Easy. You're on foot. This would be a cinch if you were in your truck.

For all of the resources he packed into his get home bag, the one thing he really could use that he did not have was a mode of transportation. Naturally, there was no way to fit anything he could ride in his bag, not even a scooter. He should have asked Doc Sam about it before he left, but he didn't even consider it. He only kept automobiles in mind. He didn't think of something much smaller, like a scooter, or a...

"Bicycle," he audibly finished.

Jacob had not ridden a bicycle regularly since he was a teenager, and even then, he pretty much had stopped by the time he was fourteen. He feared his bike would get stolen, and as he closed in on sixteen years old, he desired his own car anyway. It was mildly embarrassing that Domino had had her own car before he could buy his own, but he didn't mind after a while. He had taught his kids to learn how to ride, but he only had mounted a bike himself once or twice in his adult years.

Ironically, riding one might be the key to his survival, plus his family's. But now he had to find one. Should he go back to Trapp and ask one of the residents to borrow one? He had been on the road for two hours. That would make two hours to get back, which meant he would have wasted four hours. Riding a bike would not instantly get all that time back.

Doc Sam would understand. He'd have to.

Jacob nearly turned around on the spot, but the glimpse of a sloping roof on the horizon held him fast. There was a house up ahead. Perhaps someone was there who could help him. If the home's owner could loan him a bike, he wouldn't have to worry about wasting two more hours to return to Trapp.

With some renewed excitement, Jacob jogged to the front door of the house. It was actually a small ranch. There was a green car parked in the driveway. The wooden fence's support posts were slightly overgrown.

Jacob knocked on the front door. No response. A few more knocks did not change anything.

He checked around the sides of the house, but discovered nothing else, no vehicles, no further signs of life. Perhaps the owner was not home.

Damn.

Jacob returned to the road. So that was for nothing after all. Now he would have to turn back.

Or maybe he just could walk a little farther. Maybe another house was just a mile or two away.

He succumbed to that hope and followed the road.

In reality, it took about three miles, but he did find another house, which was another ranch. This time there was no vehicle in the driveway at all. A few cows greeted Jacob with some moos. However, there were no signs of human life. Jacob tipped his hat to the farm animals and started off again.

A third ranch lay a short hike away. This time, Jacob was greeted with a rundown house with a "for sale" sign. The lawn was overgrown and poorly kept. The only thing that greeted Jacob was a tarantula on the porch. The hairy arachnid, after facing Jacob for a moment, turned and crawled along the wall toward the end of the porch.

Let me guess. Are you the new owner of the house?

Jacob didn't stick around for long. It was plain no one was going to answer him, and a search of the property revealed no bicycle. He set back onto the road.

He was about to throw in the towel and turn around when another home off the road tempted him to continue. *Just one more*, he thought. He gritted his teeth. He had been at this "just one more" routine for a while. How much time was he throwing away by doing this?

Jacob approached the latest house. It was a nice-looking farm house, definitely better than the one he just had left. There was a red truck sitting in the driveway. The fence was largely free of foliage. The front windows, however, were boarded up. The wood looked fairly new, not worn by the weather. The owner must have put these up recently, perhaps in response to the EMP.

That would seal in the home's air, Jacob thought. Without air circulation, living in there would be mighty uncomfortable. Hell, if a fire broke out, it even could be fatal. This guy might be reacting to the terrors occurring outside, but he did not seem to know how to handle it. Jacob vowed to help him out.

Jacob knocked on the door. No response.

"Hello?" Jacob called, "Sir! I'm not here to hurt you." Jacob raised his open hands. "I'm hoping we can help each other."

The silence lingered. Jacob listened for the creak of floorboards inside, to hear if somebody was approaching the door.

Please God, let somebody be in there.

"Hello?" Jacob called a few more times, but neither that nor additional knocks drew the home's owner to the door. He might be hunkered down inside, or he may not be home.

Maybe he's around back. Jacob had not explored the sides of the house. He left the porch and checked the left side of the house.

There was nothing and nobody there. However, he did find the very thing he was looking for on the right side, parked by the side door—a bicycle!

"Thank God!" Jacob let out a long breath. At last! Now he could make up considerable ground, provided the ranch's owner would let him borrow it.

So, I have the bike, but now I need permission.

Jacob waited. A few minutes passed. No one approached. The ranch's owner did not emerge from the house. Where the hell was he?

I can't stick around here forever. I need to get going.

He eyed the bicycle with rising envy. If Jacob couldn't secure permission to take the bike, perhaps he should borrow it anyway.

You mean steal it.

The word struck Jacob in the throat. It sounded nasty. It offended him. He wasn't stealing it. He just was borrowing it. He would return it once he returned this way.

Yeah, you think you'd let your kids get away with that? You sound like one of the guys in the old neighborhood.

That thought further offended him. He was better than those guys. They were selfish assholes. He was helping his family. The difference was stark and wide.

Keep telling yourself that.

Jacob ignored his own self-nagging as he examined the bike. It was old. It was chained to the water meter than protruded from the ground. The chain wasn't that tight. Perhaps the owner owned another bike that he rode to get supplies and food. He probably didn't even care about this one.

Keep telling yourself that.

Jacob knelt down and checked the chain's knot. It was loose enough that he could untie it with a little effort.

It didn't take long to free the bike. Jacob looked at the tires. They seemed well inflated. He mounted it. The bicycle quaked a little from the rustiness of Jacob's riding skills.

C'mon, this isn't hard. You have to do this.

Jacob started pedaling. After a few strokes, old confidence filled his limbs. This wasn't too hard to remember. He didn't pedal very fast, but his speed outpaced what he had been achieving on foot.

He rode the bike away from the house and onto the road. No retaliation came his way. The owner did not roar from the home with a shotgun screaming "Thief! Robber!"

"Sorry," he said under his breath. He would return this, though. Perhaps he could accomplish this mission before the bike's owner returned to his home. The owner might not even know it was gone.

Keep telling yourself that.

Jacob scowled at his inner voice. Why should he

be so hard on himself? The times had changed. These were the choices he had to make. God knows, he would have to make difficult ones in the future.

You've always said you'd be better than the guys you left behind.

Jacob kept his eyes ahead. Perhaps the dream of those strange god-like figures rattled him. Deep down, he wasn't convinced that he *was* different.

THANKS to the bike's speed, Jacob reached the turnoff within about ten minutes. The sight of Road 219 sank Jacob's heart. Automobiles littered the road like discarded toys. Some vehicles had their doors open, their drivers and passengers having fled.

Jacob slowed down so he could peddle down the middle of the road, cutting between the stalled vehicles. It was bizarre. Yesterday the roads Jacob traveled had been lined with confused people looking for help, answers, anything. The stillness of this current scene sent shivers down his spine.

Jacob then pedaled past a four-door car that was just off the side of the road. It had smashed into a tree. The impact had crumpled the hood and engine compartment, but worse, it had killed the driver and front passenger on impact. The backs of the two unfortunate souls easily were visible, and before Jacob could stop or turn away, he pedaled within easy sight of their faces. They had smashed into the dashboard so deeply it seemed as though the foot of a giant had squashed the pair into their car.

Jacob picked up the pace to get away from the car. He felt so ill that he had to skid to a stop. He huffed and wheezed and, for a while, he thought he would throw up.

"Damn it!" he repeated through heavy breathing. The visage of those two dead people had shaken him up badly. He never had seen people so gruesomely killed, not in person. No R-rated shoot 'em up film could have prepared him for this.

It took a few minutes for Jacob to get his bearings. He felt well enough to start riding again, and he vowed to put a great amount of distance between himself and this scene in a hurry.

Middleburg. Let me get there soon.

CHAPTER ELEVEN

Doc Sam rapped on the wooden door. With the soft wind blowing through his hair, Cowell watched the door with his hands in his pockets. Though he tried to remain composed, he had remained on edge even while accompanying Doc Sam on the about forty minute walk to this fish and bait store. It probably was because the enormity of this situation finally was weighing down on him. He couldn't even feel safe in this small town.

The doctor must have read his mood on the way here, because he said, "I wouldn't worry yourself. Trapp's crime rate is one of the lowest in the state. Most of us know each other. We're a well-behaved lot." He chuckled before adding, "It's when the refugees start pouring in that we might have a problem. That's why we're going to have you set by the end of the day."

The door opened, breaking Cowell's train of

thought. A black gentleman with a white puffy beard stuck his head out of the doorframe of the fish and tackle store. "Hey, Doc!" the man bellowed with such volume that it stung Cowell's ears.

"Moses!" Doc Sam nodded to Cowell. "This here is a stray I picked up. Alexander Cowell. We need to build him a get home bag, that is, if you still got the supplies."

Moses stepped out into the sun. He rubbed his long flannel shirt, his hand grazing a yellow stain near the bottom of the shirttail. "Oh, I packed for Doomsday, baby. I have more than enough for whoever you throw at me." Chuckling, he walked toward Cowell. "Hi. Moses Travers." He offered his hand. "Lifelong Virginian."

Cowell took Moses's hand and shook it. "Pleased to meet you," Cowell said. Moses acted very friendly, despite his messy appearance. In addition to his stained shirt, he also was wearing old khakis that sported holes at the knees. As Moses walked back to his store, Cowell also took note of a limp in his right leg. Perhaps age or an ailment had struck Moses, though Cowell wondered if Moses possessed a colorful history overseas like the doctor. *Birds of a feather do flock together*, Cowell thought.

"Come in." Moses wagged his right finger. "Let's get you started, Mister Alex."

I prefer to be called Mister Cowell. However, Cowell quickly decided decorum should be the least of his worries. Doctor Sam said Moses could help, and Cowell was eager to get on with matters.

"SIT, SIT." Moses repeated it as he loaded the wooden table with a bevy of supplies.

The shop owner had led Cowell and Doc Sam into this back storeroom. Cowell coughed. The air in here was stagnant and hot. Doc Sam must have thought so too. The first thing he did was open the storeroom's only window. Fortunately, the storeroom also offered a green couch for Cowell to sit on while Moses sorted the supplies.

"So, tell me, Mister Alex, where are you trying to get to?" Moses asked. "With everyone's cars shut down, you're going to have to get there on foot."

Cowell cleared his throat. "My residence is actually in Vienna. I would like to go there if possible, but it's also close to D.C."

Doc Sam whistled loudly. "No kidding."

"Too close." Moses's eyes widened. "You're going to have scores of folks between you and there, and many of them are going to be scared shitless. I wouldn't want to be close to them when things start turning ugly."

Cowell grimaced. "Right. Yes, Doctor Samuel has told me how dangerous it would be to try going there, so I wasn't seriously entertaining it. Instead, I'd like to go to Fall Crossing."

Doc Sam raised an eyebrow. "Fall Crossing?"

"Yeah. My older sister lives there and she's the only family I have that's close by," Cowell said.

"So, you don't have a wife or kids?" Moses said.

"No. No, nobody of that sort," Cowell said, "my mother passed in January and she was divorced from my father. He lives in Florida. Last I heard my stepfather was in Connecticut, but that was a week ago. I couldn't begin to guess what happened to him."

Doc Sam hovered over Moses. "Fall Crossing is an interesting choice. It's pretty far, much closer to Richmond than up here. But that's a planned community. I'm amazed part of your flock ended up there considering you don't exactly go for people who want to live off the grid."

"Well, my sister and I never saw eye to eye on a lot of things," Cowell said.

"Planned community?" Moses turned his head to look at Doc Sam. "What's so special about that? There are planned communities all over the country."

"Well, a *special* planned community." Doc Sam picked up a water bottle from the table and stared at it. "It's not like the folks who just say, 'Hey, you can build here, but not over there, to preserve the forest?' It's a liberty community. They put out the word that they want folks who think and live a certain way to come and settle there, help build the town. In Fall Crossing, they want you to be self-reliant, value hard work and independence." He looked at Cowell with a wry grin. "In other words, you'd be knocking on *everyone's* door in that little community to get interviews with the kids."

Moses frowned. "What are you talking about?"

"Just a little joke," Doc Sam replied, "Don't mind it."

Cowell shifted in his seat. He didn't want to reveal his occupation and he was glad Doc Sam did not speak of it. Although Cowell could do without the doctor's jest that referenced his past practices with the Avery family.

"Anyway, I very much would like to get on with this," Cowell said. "Given what happened yesterday, Fall Crossing probably would be the best place for me. I'm sure you both would agree."

"I agree." Doc Sam scratched his chin. "Those folks know how to live off the grid and likely already are prepping the town for what's to come. But on foot, that'll take days to get there from here. You do know this won't be a quick jog."

"I do." Cowell straightened up. "Please, let's move on with my get home bag."

"Right." Moses patted a folded-up poncho on the edge of the table.

"Now, this is a rain poncho. Since you're going on a multi-day trip, you're almost certainly going to need this. Now, don't go thinking you just can stand out in the rain because it's just a little water on you. Too much rain can cause hypothermia. Remember, your clothes are going to stay wet for a long time. It's not like you can pop them into the dryer while you relax in a comfy bathrobe." Moses took hold of the poncho in his right hand. "This little baby will go on you real easy."

Makes sense, Cowell thought.

Moses turned to a set of what looked like cigarette lighters and a small plastic bag beside them. "Now, these are fire starting tools. Lighters and tinder. Useful for warmth and cooking food."

Cowell eyed the plastic bag. "Tinder?"

"Oh, tinder is just the material that starts the kindling burning." Moses pointed to the bag. "You don't want to be hunting around the forest looking for stuff to burn, especially if it's wet out. I know you're a babe in the woods compared to the rest of us, so we want this to go easy for you." He picked up the bag. "Rip 'her open, stick the tinder on the ground and light it with the lighter. Instant flame."

"Great," Cowell said. Short and sweet. He understood everything Moses had said so far. He was starting to feel optimistic about his chances.

Moses fished out a folded-up map from the pile. "This is pretty self-explanatory. It's a topographic map that'll tell you about forests, hills, rivers, streams, all that stuff. Trust me, this is invaluable, especially without GPSs or Google to bail you out. Comes with a compass, too." Moses then pointed to a paper pad and pen. "Since we can forget about jotting info in our phones, it's back to good old-fashioned pen and paper. This is great for writing down anything you think you ought to remember later on."

"That's very important," Doc Sam said with a note of sternness. "You may need to scratch down info on a landmark you see on the way, something you want to keep in mind later on."

As Moses brushed his hand across the table, he knocked over a small rectangular hand radio. "Whoops." He picked up the radio. "Yeah, ordinarily we'd pack one of these too."

"I know. It doesn't work anymore," Cowell said grimly.

"Actually, I packed a whole bunch of these babies away in a faraday cage." Moses switched on the radio.

Cowell's heart quickened for a moment, hoping he would hear an emergency transmission of some sort, perhaps a government official finally laying out what had happened and what the people should do. But even after turning the dial, the radio spewed nothing but crackles.

"It still might come in handy," Doc Sam said. "You have no idea who might be out there. Someone, someday, may be able to get back on the air."

Moses exhaled slowly. "You right." He set the radio back down. "We still should hold out hope, shouldn't we?"

Hope. Is that all we have to go on? Cowell bristled. He was in the middle of a situation with no ounce of certainty from any of the institutions he had been told to rely on while growing up. Now, nobody could count on the American government, the police, or the military coming to the rescue. Everything from here on depended on their—his—ability to fend off both man and elements with whatever tools or cunning existed on hand.

As Moses pushed aside some of the small clutter, his hand revealed a small pistol and a can of pepper spray. As Moses lifted his hand, it was clear he wanted to show off these two items. "Now, we have to make sure you get to Fall Crossing in one piece. Aside from Mother Nature, man might be your greatest challenge."

Cowell's stomach turned. He figured he would need weapons but viewing them did not make it any easier.

"The key is keeping anyone who's looking to make trouble away from you. If an attacker's approaching, you got to drop him before he gets close. If they got a knife, it's going to be your ass. Hell, if they got strong muscles behind their hands, you're going to be lying dead in the leaves anyway." Moses held the pistol. It was a compact weapon, smaller than any gun Cowell ever had seen in his life, yet its trigger and barrel remained a stark reminder that a gun, however small, would be a deadly one.

And he might have to use it.

"Once you reach Fall Crossing, I strongly urge you to train yourself in firearm use. Hopefully, they'll offer you shelter until you get up to speed," Moses added.

Cowell nodded. "Of course." Mentally, he laced his thoughts with sarcasm. *Get up to speed. It's like I have to relearn how to deal with the world.*

MOSES CONTINUED to show Cowell everything he would need on the trip to Fall Crossing, including packed food and a canteen to hold water, along with water bottles that would sustain him for the journey. Moses also gave Cowell a book that contained survival instructions and tips.

"This will speed things along," Moses said, "I don't have time to give you the crash course, but I think between what I told you and this little book, you'll be in good shape."

Cowell rapidly flipped through the small manual. He stopped more than once when a term or phrase confused him, such as the "gray man" theory. The book provided instructions on how to blend into a populated area, to go unnoticed by appearing to be as inconspicuous as possible to passers-by. Another page dealt with putting out a fire in the wilderness. Additional flips of the pages instructed Cowell on stringing food up in a tree to remove it from the reach of animals. The book also talked about how to recognize signs of approaching bad weather.

Damn, this book really is helpful.

He looked up. Moses already had packed up a bag. Cowell frowned. The "get home bag" was actually a large backpack. It was certainly bigger than Jacob Avery's bag. It looked more like a camping bag.

"It's, uh, certainly big," Cowell said with a nervous laugh.

"Yeah, since you're going to Fall Crossing, we decided not to take any chances with you," Moses said.

"But I'm sure this is a big imposition," Cowell said. "I'm taking a lot from you."

"Like I said before, I packed away a lot of supplies for just such an emergency. Even this won't be a major drain on my inventory." Moses set the pack on its back on the table. "But, for a haul of this size I would ask for some compensation."

"Right, right." Cowell put the book away, then fished in his back pocket for his wallet. But just as he pulled it out, he grumbled. "Oh, of course. I forgot dollar bills don't have the value they used to. What would you like me to do for you?"

"Nothing too complicated. And the good news is you can be done in less than a day." Moses marched past Doc Sam toward the back of the storeroom. "Just a moment."

Moses returned a moment later with a cardboard box. "Now, this is filled with special canteens." Moses slammed the box down on the couch seat beside Cowell. "All empty, ready to be filled. Now, you're new here, so you haven't been to Jellico's."

Cowell shook his head. "No, I haven't."

"Alright. No problem. It'll take a little walking, but you can spot it easy. Jellico's is an orchard. Since the power went out, the owner, Ian, has been arranging people to do some work there in exchange for fruits, oranges, grapes, pears, things like that.

There's also a well where you can draw water. Now, I've got an IOU with Ian, so he'll let you draw what I need. Your job's going to be twofold." Moses picked up one of the bottles. "You're going to fill these with water. I'm going to take these babies and purify the water inside them so it's suitable for drinking. Now, the second half of your job is to fetch me a crop of grapes and potatoes." He tapped his right leg. "I'm not as spry as I used to be. Just do that, and it will pay for the additional help I'm giving you."

"That doesn't sound hard, although I've never picked potatoes before or drawn water with a bucket out of a well," Cowell said.

"I'll write down some instructions to help you out. It's not difficult." Moses pulled out a pad from his front shirt pocket. Once he fished out a pen from his pants pocket, he began writing.

More stuff I have to learn, Cowell thought. Still, retrieving the water and food that Moses wanted was a fair and just payment for all that Moses had done for him. Besides, picking crops sounded like an interesting learning experience.

CHAPTER TWELVE

Jacob huffed. Even with his physically fit frame, trying to handle this bicycle exhausted him. If he had ridden a bike consistently throughout his adult years, he probably would not feel this wrung out. Only his determination to reach Middleburg kept his feet to the pedals.

Suddenly, a gust of wind buffeted him. It was so strong that he nearly fell over. Where did that come from?

Jacob realized that at some point along the way he had left the trees behind and now was riding against fully open air. The highway stretched some distance without the cover of trees, exposing it to gusts of wind. A coating of gray clouds passed by, indicating that a storm might be approaching.

Another punch of wind nearly knocked Jacob down. He put on the brakes. He was simply too exhausted to keep pedaling and stand against the wind. He would have to walk the bike across this road until the wind died down or the highway was shielded by trees again to block some of the gusts.

As he trekked down the road, his mind turned to someone he had not thought about in a while. He wondered what Sheryl was doing right now. She had to have realized that the world situation had deteriorated so badly that fleeing her hometown was her best course of action.

Jacob recalled their past conversations. He had instructed her on how to escape from a populated area that was shut down and in a state of anarchy. Make yourself invisible, for one thing. With the proper clothing, you even can make yourself look like a man to decrease the risk that a rapist or a thief will think you're an easy mark.

Sheryl had listened, though sometimes she seemed amused by her brother's words. Jacob's scenarios sounded so outlandish. How could things turn so bad? Jacob admitted he wasn't Nostradamus, that he wasn't predicting anything would happen for certain, but there was nothing wrong with preparing for a possible disaster just in case. And as Jacob pointed out, large metro areas still could suffer wide scale blackouts, as New York City had in 2003. Major storms could leave large populated areas in tatters, as Hurricane Sandy had done to New Jersey and New York in 2012.

Of course, yesterday's solar event dwarfed all of those disasters combined. Jacob hoped Sheryl had understood her current situation early on and got out before the area was engulfed in a major conflagration, either fire, riots or something worse.

His arm suddenly felt wet near the elbow. A water drop had hit his flesh. So, this area was about to receive rain after all. Jacob picked up the pace. He should try reaching cover if possible.

THE SPORADIC DROPS turned to a light drizzle, which progressed further into rain, though it never became heavy. However, by that time, Jacob had reached a place where a new line of trees paralleled the road. He could pull his bike off the road and set up a shelter.

The large branches of a nearby tree provided a strong shield from most of the rain. As long as the weather did not worsen in the next few minutes, he should have enough time to set up his tent. He needed a break to eat and drink anyway, and the occasion of the weather provided a good opportunity to stop for a rest.

After setting the bike against a tree, Jacob put down his get home bag. This bag was designed just as it was named, a way to sustain him if he should be caught away from home without a working automobile or any conventional mode of transportation. But it now had turned into a traveling bag that was meant to keep him going until he reached Middleburg and returned to Trapp. Although Doc Sam had offered to give him a bigger bag with more provisions, courtesy of Moses Travers, Jacob was satisfied that his current bag would do the trick. Besides, a lighter load made it easier for him to travel. If he carried a large backpack, he doubted he could have remained steady enough to ride the bicycle.

Setting up the tent was easy. He chose a space between two trees and strung up a rope between them. Then he used the rope as a clothesline to hang his tarp.

With a shelter in place, Jacob opened up his bag. It was built around the three cores of survival. His tent was part of the shelter core. Jacob fished out a canteen. The metal canister contained water, the second core. The third core was fire, but Jacob did not need or want to start a fire out here in the rain. He would have liked to cook one of his cans of soup, but that would have to wait. A nutritious energy bar and water would suffice.

Jacob set down a small plastic bag to sit on. He had favored these as quick cushions to sit on while out in nature. He did not want to use cloths or towels unless he had to. If they got dirty from being placed on soil or on a surface with flowing rain water, Jacob would have to clean them off in a river and hang them up to dry. A plastic surface was easier to clean.

After eating, Jacob pulled out his map and notepad. The pitter patter of rain drops did not disturb his concentration. It even had a charm to it.

He could review his progress on the map up until now without any trouble. As he studied the map, he scribbled down every sign he had passed, whether it was a mile marker or a directional sign that marked how many miles it would be to Middleburg.

Once he was satisfied that he recalled the very last sign he had passed, he looked on the map to see how much farther it would be to his destination. He worried that he had eaten up precious time looking for a bike. However, he found that his bike riding had returned much of that time to him. He would be right about here by now if he walked. So, his efforts were a wash so far. But that did not mean his bicycle couldn't earn its keep. Even with the delay caused by the rain, he still could gain a few hours if the rain stopped fairly soon and he could resume his journey.

Once he satisfied himself with that calculation, he relaxed. There was not much else to do but wait. However, he quickly grew antsy. What could he do?

A book. I could have brought one along. I can't believe I didn't think about that. Doc Sam had some books in his home and probably would have loaned one to him for the journey.

Left with little to do besides check the contents of his bag again, his thoughts drifted back to Domino and his family. He wondered how they were holding up in Trapp, and if Jubilee finally had woken up.

———

DOMINO PEERED into the room once again. Brandon had finished wiping Jubilee's face, and now he was drying it off with a clean washcloth. According to Brandon, Jubilee was shifting around in bed, having moved around a few times just in the past few hours. Doc Sam said she likely would awaken soon, and that Brandon and Domino should be ready.

I wish she could stay asleep until Jay returns. But Domino preferred that Jubilee regain consciousness as soon as possible. Domino did not like the idea of telling Jubilee that her father had left, but she wanted her to be up, alert and able to eat and drink. Domino also dearly missed hearing her daughter's voice. Seeing her asleep like this was as though she was here, but not really here.

The sound of Doc Sam's footsteps turned Domi no's head. The doctor approached from the front door. She had been so deep in thought that she had not heard him open and close the door.

"Is your little girl still in dreamland?" he asked softly.

"She is, but Brandon says she's moving more," Domino replied.

"That's good, that's good. I figured her as a tough lady." Doc Sam then nodded toward the living room. Domino took it as a cue to join him without summoning Brandon.

Doc Sam waited until he reached the longest couch before he talked. "Just wanted you to keep your guard up. I had a chat with a neighbor on the way in. There was a break-in at a hardware store on Valley Street. With the electronics dead, the alarm system was shot. He broke open the back door and made off with some tools. Drake, a policeman, was out on patrol when he saw the man, told him to stop, and then squeezed off a shot. Now, Drake isn't sure, but he thought this guy tried to shoot back. It was dark, so he couldn't see well. But the man was about..." The doctor put out his hand to about the center of his temple. "...this high. He wore dark sweats, at least that's what the witness thinks he wore. The clothes were kind of puffy. Probably clean-shaven, too."

Domino nodded. Not the kind of news she wanted to hear, but it probably should not be unexpected. Actually, she was a little surprised things were not worse.

"Just wanted you to be on the lookout. Trapp's police force still is hanging together, but they don't have computers or phones or radios. Everything is word of mouth now, person to person. So, if the burglar shows up..."

"We'll have to deal with him." Domino's hand dropped to her right hip.

Doc Sam followed her gaze. "Yeah, I see you're carrying."

Domino looked down at her belt. A handgun lay holstered on the right side of her belt.

"How long have you had it?" the doc asked.

"A few years," Domino replied. "I've had an everyday carry just about all of my adult life."

"Ever had to use it?" Doc Sam asked.

"Practice," Domino said.

"But never on a person."

Domino stared at her weapon. "Not this one."

The doctor craned his head to look at Domino's left side. "And that's not the only one you're sporting."

Domino turned her head left. The doctor had taken notice of the knife holstered on the left side of her belt. "Yeah, that too. Funny thing about a knife is you never have to reload it. I've learned how to use it, to fight with it."

"Fighting with knives is ugly as hell." Doc Sam looked up at Domino, his eyes appearing a little sad. "I've seen what a sharp blade can do to a man. It's nothing that you can forget."

"From when you served?" Domino asked.

"That and my time helping people to set up communities. In southeast Asia, Doctor Nguyen and I came across victims of a Communist militia." Doc Sam held up three fingers. "Three people without their heads. And the job was fresh. They were on their knees, hands tied behind their backs. Days after that, Nguyen decided to head back to the States."

"I'm sorry," Domino said. "I guess I shouldn't ask about your past."

"Don't worry. The sad part is, all that time overseas probably has prepared me for the hell that came yesterday. A long stretch of life that made me what I am. It's probably that way for all of us."

Domino folded her arms. "Sometimes. Sometimes it just takes one moment in time."

"Really?" Doc Sam smiled. "Happened that way with you?"

"It did. You'd never have known I was going to be..." She raised her right leg, showing off the holster that sheathed a second knife on her boot. "...well, who I am right now, if you met me when I was fourteen."

Doc Sam nodded. "I guess whatever happened sure changed your outlook on life. I guess you probably don't want to talk about it, huh?"

Domino put her foot down. "Not really. Sorry. It's just too personal."

"That's all right." Doc Sam strolled around her toward the kitchen. "Some stories aren't meant to be told to just anyone."

DOMINO WATCHED the doctor walk into the kitchen. She felt somewhat guilty for holding back her tale when Doc Sam revealed something from his past, but she couldn't bring herself to do it. The story was not an easy one to tell, not just because it was emotionally difficult, but Domino also felt that moment in time simply could not be put into spoken words. Or at the very least, she could not verbalize the impact of that moment.

As Domino had told Doc Sam, there are moments that make a person who they are. For her, that moment arrived during a dance at her high school in her freshman year. The school was a fancy place for upper income families in the D.C. metro area to send their children. Domino had graduated from a junior high school that she liked a lot and believed the expansive high school would be even better.

The dance was a fall event, hosted in late October of that year. Domino was dressed in an expensive light pink dress, puffed up with a single petticoat underneath. However, as the dance progressed, Domino thought the event was nothing to write home about. None of the guys there intrigued her. Some of the male students, however, did think something of her, for Domino spotted the wandering eyes of a couple of the guys every now and then.

As the clock approached nine, Domino grew restless. The conversations were vacuous, and she had eaten from all the dishes she had wanted. She decided to text the man who her parents hired as her driver to have him come around to bring her home.

So, she walked outside.

Without warning, Robert Halleck, one of the school football team's running backs, approached her. Domino's neck was bathed with the putrid smell of alcohol. Halleck either had snuck in some booze or received some from friends on campus. With his curly red hair and freckled cheeks, Halleck was known as a charmer among Domino's classmates. For her part, Domino didn't think much of him.

She thought even less of Halleck when he grabbed her skirt and yanked it up, exposing her underwear.

Domino, enraged, yanked her garment back down while stomping on Halleck's right foot. He screamed a profanity as he limped back a step.

"Asshole!" Domino screamed at him.

She turned and ran off, but Halleck suddenly broke into a run and caught up with her. He seized her by her arms and tried kissing her. She slapped him hard. Halleck, his eyes widening, threw her down to the grass.

Domino's hand knocked against a discarded glass soda bottle. It was within easy reach. As Halleck dropped down to his knees, Domino grabbed the bottle and smashed it against his head.

Halleck, yelling in pain, braced the side of his head. Blood trickled down his face. Domino hit him three more times until he fell onto his back. Domino climbed to her feet and shouted for help.

Her four smacks to Halleck's head earned him a trip to the hospital. Domino's parents soon arrived at the school to console her.

DOMINO WANTED action taken against Halleck. She waited and waited for any news on the matter.

However, she didn't receive any word back. Domino had not noticed anything had changed until she realized she had not spotted Halleck around school since the dance. Finally, she asked her parents if they knew anything. They replied that they just had learned that he had transferred to another school, but they did not know where.

It took weeks for Domino to learn the details. Halleck quietly left the school and, supposedly, started attending an elite school in New York. Halleck was the nephew of a Maryland congressman, and the move was made so the congressman would not be embarrassed by the revelation that his nephew had tried to rape a high school freshman. Later, Domino learned some more details. Apparently, Congressman Halleck had taken up residence in Virginia and didn't even own a home in Maryland. As Domino's source pointed out, any elected official is in deep shit and ineligible to hold office, when the folks back home learn that their "representative" doesn't even live among them any longer.

So, Domino's attacker had the good fortune to be part of a political family. He likely never would be confronted with this incident again unless Domino made a public spectacle of it, something her parents cautioned her against. Why put herself through that kind of humiliation? It was better to let the matter go.

Domino knew she got lucky back then. She might not be so lucky again. She understood the strength disparity between a man and a woman would leave her at a major disadvantage if faced with another male attacker. What could equalize that disparity?

A loaded gun, that's what.

When Domino first voiced the desire to carry around a firearm to her parents, they laughed it off. Why should she need a gun? In the kind of life she was to enjoy, at the opulent events and parties she would attend, she would enjoy armed protection. Besides, she lived in a safe neighborhood behind the walls of a gated community. She just was rattled by the incident. It would pass.

However, Domino did not let go of her desire to carry a weapon. Her parents' amusement grew to annoyance. Then, when she started investigating how to train in firearm use, her parents responded angrily. Their social circles were filled with people who supported gun restrictions. And their daughter wanted to own a gun? Not while she lived under their roof!

Domino pointed out that at least half of their friends owned a gun, despite their support of gun control. That earned her a grounding for that night. Apparently, speaking against the hypocrisies of the elite was a punishable offense.

Convincing her parents of her desire was a fool's errand. She investigated firearm use and ownership anyway. As soon as she was old enough, she had started buying and training with her own guns. The 9mm she carried was actually the third gun she ever had purchased.

That assault, that single moment in time, changed her life forever. It taught her that she could not always depend on the institutions of society to come to her rescue. The aftermath of Halleck's attack only cemented that lesson.

If she had had a gun on her that night, Halleck would not have made his escape to New York. In all likelihood, he would be dead, assuming he didn't run away at the sight of the gun. Many bullies were cowards. When faced with real force, they back off.

But not all of them.

The breakdown of society would signal to thieves, rapists and anarchists all across this land that the time was right for them to unleash their hidden desires upon the world. With no police or military to stop them, they would steal, rape and kill with impunity.

And Jacob's out in the middle of it...

CHAPTER THIRTEEN

JACOB TOOK DOWN THE SHELTER. The rain had lasted for a little more than an hour. Jacob had hesitated to remove his shelter covering and pack up until he was certain the rain had passed by, but as the sunlight increased, he felt confident he could begin his journey again.

He let out a contented sigh. The rain had given him a chance to rest and eat, so he could approach the rest of the trip with renewed energy.

Unfortunately, as he wheeled his bike back to the road, he discovered a new problem. The asphalt now was freshly wet. He would have to pedal on a watery road, causing havoc on the brakes. Also, puddles lay in places where the road sank, sloped or had small holes. He feared that if he rode through them, his bike's front wheel would catch in a pothole and fling him over the handlebars onto the nearby grass or worse, onto the street itself.

Those fears kept him from mounting his bicycle right away. Even when he rode a bike regularly years ago, he rarely pedaled on wet roads. Generally, he did not travel very much during times of rain. He often stayed in one spot, whether to relax, do schoolwork, or hang with friends.

But if I stay on foot, I won't reach Middleburg before the sun goes down. Whether he liked it or not, he had to try.

So, Jacob remounted his bike and started pedaling, though his pace remained slow. Would his wheels slip and slide? Would he skid off the road and into the grass? Fear kept him in the center of the road and at a relatively slow speed. By staying at the road's highest point, he avoided puddles and water runoffs.

After a while, Jacob's apprehension started to fade. The lack of motorized traffic meant he could stay in the middle of the road without worry, and since this road led straight to Middleburg, he was spared major turns that might upset his balance.

As his confidence grew, Jacob couldn't help but feel amazed. He never thought up until last night that he would pedal from one town to another, to say anything about riding through a freshly rained-on road. Life had thrown challenge after challenge his way, and he had taken each one and adapted to it.

But that's how life has been, hasn't it? That's how you wanted it.

Indeed, Jacob had decided on that course when

he was eighteen. That was his seminal moment, the time that made him who he was. He was on the verge of graduating high school. Sheryl, four years older than him, had come visiting from medical school. She wanted Jacob to come with her to Pleasantville, where she was studying and would complete her work. She believed Jacob should go to college there and become an engineer.

Sheryl cared for Jacob. She knew his life on the streets had been difficult and at times life-threatening. She imagined a new life for him, one that put him in coveralls working on a power transmission line and perhaps in time in a suit and a tie. She saw him as a smart, hardworking man who could achieve great things.

At the same time, their mother was ill. She had been sickly since Jacob had been a high school junior. She was approaching sixty and never had been in robust health. Sheryl wanted to uproot her as well and take her to Pleasantville. They would be one big, happy family there.

Jacob was tempted. He almost took Sheryl up on it. But the lure of another life called to him.

Domino first had brought it to his attention. She had been looking up pictures of country houses when she found an account of how the family who resided in one of them lived their life. It was fascinating. The family had chosen to live off the grid. They grew their own food and canned it for long-term storage.

Domino showed Jacob the online link to the story, and he became fascinated by it. He wanted to learn more.

Within a couple of months, Jacob had consumed a lot of information about how to live in a rural setting in a self-sufficient manner. It was as if he had discovered a gateway to a whole other world. He could escape the dark influences that marked his teenage years in Alexandria, the rowdy and unruly teens who tried to get him into trouble and often thrashed him for not going along with them.

Better yet, he could spare his children the same fate. If he raised them out in the countryside, he would not have to worry about them falling in with a malicious crowd.

When he first broached the idea to Sheryl, she laughed. She thought he was indulging in a fanciful dream that he soon would discard in favor of her "wise" plan for his life. Admittedly, he did not dismiss it out of hand. He appreciated what Sheryl would do for him.

In the end, Jacob still would reside in a heavily populated urban setting. Even if he had lived in a more upscale area, he couldn't shake the feeling that the shadows of his old life would come back to haunt him or his kids, if he had any. He just didn't want to take the chance any longer. He yearned to make a clean break.

And so, one day, Jacob told Sheryl of his plans to buy a home far from the city.

At first, Sheryl took it as a joke that was going too far, but once she figured out Jacob was serious, she launched into a series of questions about Jacob's choice. Where would he get the money to build his so-called dream life? How would he educate his children? Could Domino really handle all that he planned to accomplish? What about medical needs? Would he live close enough to a hospital?

In fact, given that Sheryl was going into the medical field, she peppered Jacob with many questions about how he could endure the rural life, from handling animals to venomous bites from insects or snakes. Jacob answered some, but not all of Sheryl's concerns. He admitted he had to do further research about living off the grid. He didn't plan to launch into it right away, but from what he read, he felt confident he could pull it off.

"You don't know what you're getting into," Sheryl had told him. "You won't be safer out there. If you have an emergency, it'll take longer for the police to reach you."

She also could not understand what kind of a living Jacob would pursue. If he went to college, he could end up with a well-paying career that would give him any home he wanted. Would Jacob make enough in his current position in life to pay for his rustic homestead and whatever else he needed?

"Domino has a big stipend from her parents. They don't talk very much anymore, but they still wanted to give her something to get on her feet,"

Jacob had told Sheryl. "With a year or two of work, I can make more than enough to buy a house and get started."

Sheryl couldn't see it. In her mind, Jacob was leaping off a high cliff without a bungee cord and expecting to fly safely down to the ground.

As much as it pained him, Jacob knew the two of them would part and live in different areas of the state. Sheryl had, almost miraculously, stayed out of the hard life of Alexandria's streets. Jacob admired her for that. She was too smart to get involved with the wrong crowd. But her intellect also kept her from entertaining an alternative to the city life she always had known.

Jacob wasn't asking Sheryl to join him. He readily accepted her life choices. She just seemed so uneasy with the idea in general that it cast a pall over their relationship. After their mother had passed away a few years ago, it seemed they had even less reason to talk.

We may never get another chance to talk, he thought. If the worst had occurred, if she had been caught in the aftermath of the EMP blackout and was killed, they never would have the opportunity to reconcile their differences.

DOMINO PEERED into the small room where Jubilee slept. Brandon was inside once again, but he was not tending to his sleeping sister. Instead he sat nearby and just stared at her. He dug his hands into his pants pockets, his tension evident. Domino wondered what was wrong.

"Hey." She walked up to him, speaking quietly. "You haven't left this room except to use the bathroom." She chuckled. "I guess Doctor Sam's little piping system hasn't caused any problems."

Last night, the doctor showed them his homemade piping system that ran into his bathroom, which would take away waste without the assistance of Trapp's plumbing system. It was a great source of relief for the Averys and for Cowell. Brandon had joked about having to go outside from now on to relieve themselves, much to Cowell's chagrin.

"Nope. I pee, I press the handle, it goes down the pipe," Brandon said, quickly and without much energy.

"Now you don't sound much like the Brandon I know." Domino knelt down by him. She started nuzzling his hair. "My son who is full of energy and gloriously creative observations on life."

Brandon sighed. "I don't know. Maybe..." He drew his legs closer in under his chair. "I just wish I had seen that creep sneaking up with the bow and arrow."

"Aww, you're thinking you could have stopped Jubilee from being shot?" Domino wrapped her arm around Brandon's shoulders. "Sweetie, you couldn't have known he was there. You were fishing with your sister. You were having fun. He shouldn't have been on our land at all."

"I know," Brandon replied.

"If anything, I think your father and I dropped the ball. We probably should have put up motion sensors, but I was afraid the damned—sorry, stupid--thing would go off every time a bird flew over our fence. He thought we should set up cameras, maybe link the alarm to that, but..." Domino threw up her hands. "Well, that's one problem we don't have anymore."

"That's something else. I miss using my phone. I miss watching TV. I'll never be able to stream *Star Wars* again. And Jubes won't have her MMA anymore." Brandon rested his elbows on his legs and propped up his hands in his palms. "I know everything's terrible and I shouldn't think about, you know, watching movies."

"It's alright. I think we're all a little shocked and, yes, we're thinking about the fun things that we're not going to have anymore. But you are thinking about your sister, about how to survive. You have a good heart." Domino kissed the side of Brandon's head. "It's natural to mourn the fun things. But we still can find things to do. I mean, you and your sister fish in our lake. You two know how to enjoy yourselves outside. Some things in your life aren't going to change."

A small smile formed on Brandon's lips. "Yeah," he said.

"And, you and your sister can find new things to enjoy. You have a great imagination. Why not write a story? You can't take away pencils and paper with a big electromagnetic pulse, can you?"

Brandon's smile grew. "Nope."

"And you also can draw things. We can find colored pencils, markers, crayons. Those aren't electronic. Put whatever is in your head down on paper. Draw stuff that can really knock our socks off."

Now Brandon grinned. "Sure." He pulled free from Domino's hold and stood up. "And I know what I want to draw. I want to draw this house!"

"Really?" Domino stood up.

"It's so weird! It's a house made of bags! I've never seen a house like this before!" His smile faded a little. "My phone doesn't work, so I can't take any pictures. I want to remember this place when we leave."

Domino agreed. She too wanted to have something to remember this home by. "Well, let's find you something to draw with. Maybe Doctor Sam has something you can use."

As Domino escorted Brandon out of the room, she thought about Doc Sam himself. The man produced a lot of warm feelings inside her, perhaps because he was like a father figure. Domino's relationship with her own father had run hot and cold, and during the last few years, she did not know his or her mother's whereabouts at all. So, she probably had lost any opportunity of reconnecting with her parents, if she desired to do so.

If they're still alive, what do they think now? Do they understand what's happened? Are they thinking of me now? And how would they be able to survive? How would anyone survive if they had not learned the kind of survival skills that she and Jacob studied?

CHAPTER FOURTEEN

COWELL SLAMMED the pack down on the ground before sitting down next to it. He was spent. He had tried. He put all he could into picking the grapes, but he still only had picked half of the amount Moses wished.

It's my damn fault. I should have done this first. I figured drawing the water would be easier, get it out of the way.

Sweat coated almost all of his shirt and much of his pants. Simply being outside, exposed to the sun, wore him down. He craved the presence of a functioning air conditioner. Sometimes he believed all he had to do was go inside to cool off, to replenish his energies so he could return outside, only to recognize that no working HVAC was going to await him and that there was no point. He might as well keep working.

He looked at his dirty hands. They had not been

so caked with soil since he was a child. He always had worked in clean environments. He poured himself into academic studies, progressing through college up to government jobs and eventually into an independent practice, though the government still retained his services when needed. Nothing in his life had prepared him for this.

Josephine, she's a different story. He and his sister were as different as night and day. *And to think, I have to go to her and plead for shelter. We haven't spoken in two years. What will she say to me?*

Cowell watched a pair of young men work the crops, gathering their own portions inside brown sacks slung over their shoulder. They had been working longer than he had without taking a long break. Their physiques were more muscled, more fit. Cowell thought about his abdomen and noted, to his chagrin, that his once thin frame had put on a few pounds in recent months.

He wanted to get up and resume his chores so he could acquire the supplies from Moses, but exhaustion kept him rooted to the ground.

Before long, one of the men strolled by, shouldering a sack of potatoes. "Hey, man. You okay?"

"Just..." Cowell abruptly coughed before he could finish. His throat was drier than he thought. "Just resting."

"You know, you really ought to wear a hat out here. It gets hot around this time."

Cowell looked up higher and took note of the

straw hat that the man wore. The hat must help in keeping off the sunlight.

"Everybody knows that," the man said with a chuckle, exposing his teeth as he laughed.

Cowell scowled. *Hardly general knowledge where I come from*, he thought.

"Hey, if you need a drink, you can go inside *Saburo's*." The man pointed to the right, past the edge of the crop field, to a small shack across the street. "They got water in there and *Saburo's* is offering one drink free to everyone's who working."

"Really?" That offer was enough to induce Cowell's body to stand. "Thank you for telling me."

WITH HIS PACK on his back, Cowell stepped through the open doorway. The glass door was propped open, no doubt to help the room's air circulation. Most of the tables were taken up, and all of them by men. Some of them guzzled water from glasses. Just about every man had at least someone to talk to, so the room was abuzz with chatter and guffaws.

It's like the Old West, Cowell thought.

Cowell approached the counter. A thin teenage boy with an open shirt was manning it. "Hey, sir. You want water, we got it."

"I certainly could use some, young man. I would tip you, but I'm afraid it wouldn't be of any use to you," Cowell said.

The teen reached behind the bar and hoisted a glass of water. To Cowell's delight, the glass was tall. *Saburo's* was not skimping Trapp's workers.

After taking the glass, Cowell surveyed the room. The place offered a few empty tables. Cowell was happy to take one. He didn't know any of these men, so sitting with them would be too uncomfortable an experience. In any case, they didn't seem like his type of company. Of course, he held no disdain for working men. He simply never had lived in their world and felt like a stranger in their midst. He never knew what he could talk about? The latest football game? Women? Given that he cared little for sports and found open discussion of gender relations an uncomfortable subject, he doubted he would fit in at all.

Cowell took long sips of his water at a table near the window. Leaning back in the chair, he looked outside. The window overlooked a passing road, and as usual, no cars drove by. The silence of the outdoors had been eerie for the past day, but now Cowell was finding it calming. At least he was adjusting to something in this new life.

"Good afternoon."

Cowell was so startled he nearly spilled his glass. A newcomer, a tall man, had approached him. Cowell did not hear him arrive amid the conversations ringing out around him. Quickly, he composed himself. "Afternoon."

The stranger, with his brawny build, buttoned-up

red checkered shirt, blue jeans, and brown boots, looked like he could have come out of a Chuck Norris film. The neatly trimmed brown beard certainly added to the man's rustic image. "You must be from out of town," the newcomer said.

"Vienna, although I work farther south," Cowell said.

"Really? You must have been caught on the highway." The man grasped the backboard of the chair opposite Cowell. "Mind if I join you?"

Cowell figured he had been alone with his thoughts for too long. "Go ahead."

The man sat down. "Jimmy Sykes, manager of Corbin Transportation Lines, Virginia division." He offered his hand.

"Alexander Cowell." Cowell shook Sykes's hand. "Social worker, employee for the Virginia court system."

"Really? Part of the legal system, are you? You haven't worked on any cases against Corbin Transportation, have you?"

Cowell shuffled a little. "No."

Sykes chuckled. "That's a little joke. I figured by the looks of your clothes that you were probably in some high-end line of work."

Cowell tugged at his shirt. He still was wearing his button-up shirt and dress pants, and while they had started out yesterday clean and neatly pressed, by now they were dirty and ripped in a few places.

"So, you don't live in Trapp? What are you going to do? You need a place to stay, right?" Sykes asked.

"I have family in Fall Crossing, but I need supplies to get there," Cowell said.

"You're going to hike all the way there?" Sykes asked.

"I don't have a choice. I don't have any other family I can reach." Frustration boiled up inside Cowell. "Moses Travers and Doctor Samuel still think it'll be three days at least, maybe more."

"Doctor Samuel? He's that kind of eccentric man, lives in a house all made of bags of sand?" Sykes said.

"That's him," Cowell said.

"How'd you come by him?" Sykes asked.

"I was following up on a case, a family that lives off the grid. I was attempting to interview their daughter and that's when my car stalled on Road 215. I followed the family to Trapp, and soon after I met Doctor Samuel. He took me in for the night. He's been helping me get on my way."

Sykes nodded. He placed his elbows on the table and leaned in a little closer. "You don't feel very confident that you'll make it to Fall Crossing, do you?"

Cowell's frustration continued festering. "I don't know what the hell I'm doing. I am completely unprepared to handle this...this emergency. I'm not a damn farmer. I don't know anything about camping, hunting, picking corn, drawing water, braving a wilderness..." He winced. "Having to fight off and kill another human being who wants your supplies."

Sykes said nothing.

Cowell locked eyes with his companion. "How in the world did nobody see this coming? Why didn't they prepare us? I am completely lost here. And pretty soon I'm going to have to trek halfway down this state, without a car, without a working phone, anything to help me. So, yeah, I don't think I have a chance in hell of making it to Fall Crossing. I can't turn to anybody, not the mayor of this godforsaken town, not the police, not the U.S. government." Cowell clenched his fists. "I don't know what to do."

Sykes nodded. "That's a pretty powerful sentiment. I totally can understand where you're coming from. In fact, I probably would be where you are if I hadn't grown up out here in the countryside. I took a lot of lessons with me as I moved up the corporate ladder. One of those lessons was to be in command of your own destiny."

"Well, no one's in command of their own destiny any longer," Cowell said.

"Is that so?" Sykes raised an eyebrow.

Cowell frowned. What was Sykes trying to imply here? The man was a fool if he thought anyone held a tight grip over their future any longer.

"You think you can't get to Fall Crossing? What if I told you that you could make it there inside of a day?"

"How?" With a chortle, Cowell started gulping water.

Sykes leaned even closer, about halfway across the

table, and spoke in a quieter tone. "I got a working truck."

Cowell swallowed some water down the wrong pipe. After a bout of coughing, he asked, "What?"

"Easy. Don't make a big spectacle."

Cowell wiped water from his mouth. "Sorry. I mean, how the hell do you have a working truck? They all should be out of commission!"

"Hold on a second. Yeah, it's true that an electromagnetic pulse can take out the electrical systems of automobiles, but not the older ones. The ones that don't have electronics, they still can run. Basically, some 1970's and any vehicle from the 1960's or earlier are the best. They're not very common." Sykes patted his upper chest.

"Now, we at Corbin, we've been keeping an eye on the recent solar disturbances. We figured, hey, maybe there would be hits in the atmosphere, maybe some low-level pulses that would take out a town or two. Now, we missed the mark by miles, but we still prepared anyway. We switched to our oldest trucks. I came down here in one of them yesterday." Sykes took a glance at the other tables before continuing. "Of course, I'm not advertising that, for understandable reasons."

Cowell dropped his voice. "They would mob you if they knew."

"Correct," Sykes said.

"Then why are you telling me? Why are you

offering me a ride? Aside from money, and money's now worthless, what could I give you in return?"

"You have it in good with Doc Sam, right? What does he have on hand?"

"Well, I know he has a lot of medical equipment, bandages, antibiotics, anesthesia..."

"What about fuel? Gas? Oil?" Sykes asked.

"Well, I don't know. I think he mentioned something about keeping gas for a generator." Cowell snapped his fingers. "I think he might have some in his garage. Yeah, he mentioned it yesterday. But why do you ask? Do you want to trade for it?"

"Trade would not be the word I'm thinking of. I'd call it an extended loan from him to me."

Cowell stiffened. Extended loan? That didn't sound legitimate to him. "Extended loan?" Cowell asked.

Sykes's smile suddenly seemed a little sinister. "Well, maybe you could say we are appropriating the fuel for a worthy cause, namely mine."

Cowell wanted to change this subject, and fast. "What about the gas stations?"

"There's only three in town and the government took control of those quick. No way we could fuel up from one of those. A lot of stations probably are emptied by now. They're still talking that they can rig up a generator and use the gas for that." Sykes chuckled. "Bunch of fools they are."

Cowell now was fretting for a way to exit this

conversation gracefully. It was clear now that Sykes was a thief, and Cowell wanted no part of whatever he was up to. "So, you're out of gas, is that what you're saying?"

"Hell no. I got more than enough to get out of Trapp. I want to stock up on enough gas to take me anywhere I want in this country."

The impish look in Sykes's eyes continued unnerving Cowell. "I see."

"You're not sure about me, are you? I can see it in your eyes. But you're still listening, still thinking about it. I know why. It's just what you said earlier. You're lost in this new world. You don't know shit about how to survive and you're afraid you'll be dead inside of the next three days."

Sykes drew back a little. "Remember that little lesson I spoke about? Being in command of your own destiny? Here's how it works. 'He who has the gold makes the rules.' That gold can be anything. Right now, it's fuel. I want it. I'm gathering all I can before I steal away to my next target. Anyone who's with me can reap the reward."

Cowell cleared his throat. "I've noticed a lot of people around here have guns. I don't think they'll settle for arresting a thief and reading him his Miranda rights..."

"Oh, horseshit. You're going to let that stop you? Procuring my fuel isn't going to be a complicated operation. Just fill up on the gas and bring it out to the road. I'll set the time. We'll be there to pick you up. And if you're worried about someone taking a shot at you, well, I got some friends who will help us out."

Cowell bristled. As much as he hated what this guy was proposing, he couldn't stop considering it. Hell, a part of him even liked it. A chance to ride to Fall Crossing inside of a day? He'd be a fool to turn that down! Even so, just who was this guy and why should Cowell trust him?

"You talk a very good game, but I have no proof I can trust you. You could be leading me down a primrose path, only to yank the carpet out from under me. I didn't get to where I am by being gullible."

"Hey, I totally understand." Sykes nodded. "You don't have to agree to anything right now. Just keep it in mind. Keep it in mind as you toil out there and watch this world pass by, and you recognize that you don't have a place in it anymore. If you change your mind, you can look for me here."

Sykes then rose from his seat, smiled, and walked away.

Cowell, believing that was the last he would see of Sykes, let out a long sigh. Stealing from another person? That would make him no better than the dregs of this world who thought themselves free to take whatever they wanted now that all authority had broken down. Alexander Cowell was better than that. He raised the glass to his lips and prepared to drink heavily.

The glass was empty.

CHAPTER FIFTEEN

Brandon was so immersed in his latest drawing that he did not notice Doc Sam approach until the older man's shadow dwarfed his paper. "Oh, excuse me." The doctor chuckled. "Didn't mean to get into your light." He backed away from the window, allowing the sunlight to shine fully into the room. "Your mother told me what you've been up to today."

"Yeah." The nine-year-old looked up. "It's okay if I draw your house, right?"

Doc Sam laughed. "Of course! Bet you'll never see one like this ever again, although stranger things have happened."

"Why did you build your house out of bags?" Brandon asked.

"I suppose for the same reason Michelangelo carved David out of marble. He felt the need to do it, to express himself." Doc Sam grinned.

"Actually, my reason isn't quite so inspirational, I

guess. You see, when I was in Asia, I met people who didn't have a lot of money, so they didn't have homes like we do over here. They had to use branches, sticks, mud, and sometimes the homes had trouble standing up. When Doctor Nguyen and I met with some of these people, we showed them how to pack sand and dirt into bags, just like these." He pointed to the walls. "We gave them a little engineering perspective to keep the bags fortified. Last I heard, those houses they built were still in good shape."

Doc Sam cleared his throat before continuing. "Not long after I came home, I felt something was wrong just living in that apartment of mine. I was thinking of buying my own home, but that city I was in, nothing felt right. When I came back here after so many years, the first thing I noticed was this plot of land. I saw the soil, I saw the plants, and I just knew I had found my true home." He smiled wryly.

"It was also very cheap. The gentleman who sold it to me told me I was out of my mind to want to build here. He said the plumbing alone would take a lot of money to fix. So, I just built my own plumbing system. When the power went out, losing the town's plumbing wasn't a big loss."

Brandon chuckled. Doc Sam, laughing a little, stepped up to one of the living room's support beams, where he could get close to the bags that made up the front wall. "But most of all, I wanted to share in the experience of those people I left behind. This house helped me do that." He glanced at Brandon.

"It'd be nice if you had some pictures to remember this place by."

Before Brandon could speak, a series of loud horns rattled the nearby window. Doc Sam rushed to the farthest window, the one looking out on the street. A man was off in the distance, his hand raised. He was holding something, and although Doc Sam could not see it well, he knew what it was. "Damn. Air horns. The warning system."

Brandon leapt from his seat. "What's going on?"

Doc Sam sped over to the boy. "Without phones, the police honk horns to show that trouble's coming and to get ready. I think your mom's outside." The doctor fled to his office.

"Best for you to stay in here until I give the all clear." Then he emerged with a shotgun and a pair of binoculars. He quickly handed the latter to the boy. "Keep your eyes peeled. With these, you'll see trouble coming from a distance."

Brandon took the binoculars. "Will do."

COWELL STOPPED TO REST, again. Making it back to Doc Sam's was proving to be the hardest leg of this whole trip. After dropping off his crops and water at Moses Travers store, he bid Moses farewell and departed for the doctor's home. Doc Sam already had taken Cowell's gear and moved it to his home, so

Cowell was spared the ordeal of hauling it back himself.

Unfortunately, his body wanted to relax after the hard day's work, and that didn't cooperate very well with all the walking. Cowell was in a mental fight with his own legs. He had been laboring hard. Why didn't he just rest in Moses Travers store? Moses even had offered to let him sit and recuperate for a while in the backroom.

Because, once again, Cowell was too stubborn for his own good. He fumed. He still overestimated his own limits, even as he bemoaned his inability to fit into this new world. Sykes's offer looked more tempting as he thought about it.

Forget about that. The man's either talking hot air or he's a hoodlum and you shouldn't be involved with that anyway. Besides, he never would steal from another human being, not even in these dire circumstances. He simply would have to brave the open road to reach his sister.

He reached an intersection. A simple turn to the right would take him onto the street that ran past Doc Sam's house. "Almost there," he said through a dry throat.

However, he did not get more than a few steps before he heard a succession of blaring horns. They reminded him of horns that spectators would honk at a sports game. Why the hell were people shooting off horns?

Whatever the reason, the noise was enough to

unnerve Cowell and motivate his limbs to walk a little faster.

Unfortunately, his increased speed was not enough to carry him all the way to the house before trouble showed up—fast. A man dressed in sweats approached from behind, running on the opposite side of the street. He was huffing hard. Cowell soon spotted the reason why this stranger might be running. He was gripping a handgun in his right hand.

The armed man quickly closed the gap between himself and Cowell. Cowell locked eyes with him. The man's brown eyes flared with the intensity of a predatory animal. The gunman slowed quickly. His eyes widened. He saw something in Cowell, something worth taking.

Cowell's heart quickened. *Run! Get the hell out of there!* His mind screamed a host of instructions that his legs would not obey. This man had a gun. Cowell would be dead if he tried to run. *No, you fool, get away from him! You won't have a chance if you stay!*

Cowell did turn and run, but sheer terror got the better of him. He tripped and fell in the sandy ground just off the shoulder of the road.

"Cowell! Keep down!" shouted Domino.

Cowell looked up. Domino was charging in from the direction of Doc Sam's house, her gun in hand and aimed over Cowell's head. The gunman, who had slowed down almost completely, turned and ran in the opposite direction.

Domino fired the gun three times. Cowell winced

with each gunshot. He never had been so close to a discharged firearm before. The sound was much louder than he expected.

The gunman disappeared around the corner of an old shed. As Domino fired off her third shot, Doc Sam approached with his own gun in hand.

"Cowell! Quick, get inside and keep watch over the kids. Don't let them out!" Doc Sam sped off across the street. "Young lady, back me up and call out loud!"

Domino followed the doctor. "Hey!" she screamed, "Gunman outside! Watch it!"

Cowell, still planted on the ground, watched the two dash off after the gunman. He was safe, but damn, that was close—too close.

RECLINING ON THE SOFA, Cowell kept a nervous eye on the front door. He wondered what news Doc Sam or Domino would bring when they stepped through the door. Did anyone in town manage to catch the gunman?

For a moment he glanced at Brandon. The young Avery boy wore a belt that included a firearm. Cowell grimaced. Why the hell should a boy be walking around with a gun? It repulsed Cowell to think times were so bad that *children* had to walk around armed.

God help me, what would happen if someone barged into this house right now? This child is my last line of defense?

Cowell had a gun on his person thanks to Doc Sam, but he had little confidence in his ability to use it.

Figures approached the home. Cowell saw them through the window. "Mom! Doc Sam!" Brandon called. He had identified them before Cowell could. Cowell sighed in relief.

The two adults opened the front door and walked in. Doc Sam was wiping his forehead with a small cloth. "I don't envy their task in the morning, burying that son of a bitch."

Brandon rejoined his mother. She reached down and hugged him. Cowell kept silent until she stood up. "I am happy to say the time around here passed without incident," he said with a stutter.

"Good." Domino leaned over Cowell. "Thanks. Are you doing better?"

"Still a little shook up, but otherwise I can't complain," Cowell replied, "The gunman, what happened to him?"

"Reichert. He's the second in command to the sheriff. He and his posse intercepted the man and put him down." Doc Sam pushed down with his palm. "He was limping a little. Domino's gun must have put a slug in his leg. Lucky for us. It slowed him down, allowed us to catch him."

Cowell sank back into the couch. The menace of that madman was over. However, he wondered how many days would be like this. "I suppose," he said, "it is fortunate that Miss Avery was armed."

"Always carry. That's been the story of my life for

more than ten years." Domino patted her belt between her buckle and her holster.

"That's the way it's going to have to be," Doc Sam said. "There's no dialing 9-1-1 any longer." He pointed to Domino. "You were fortunate she was packing. I don't know what that bastard would have done if he thought he could do as he wished."

A cold chill ran down Cowell's back. *I could be dead by now*, he thought.

Doc Sam looked out the window. "It will be dark before too long. I'd better start thinking of what to cook for tonight." He smiled at Cowell. "After all, I do have you as a dinner guest for one more night."

"Of course." Cowell stood up, but his legs shook unexpectedly. His body was not relaxed yet. "I should run to *Saburo's*. I need to take care of some business before night falls."

"Sure," Doc Sam said.

Cowell excused himself and walked out the front door. Once in the doctor's front yard, he nearly buckled. He grabbed onto his upper legs for support.

"Damn," he said, "there's no way. There's no way I can go out there by myself." Marching into a wilderness for three days with no one else around to help him was a fool's errand. He knew it.

And so, his choice, uncertain as it had been for the past few hours, became crystal clear.

Cowell shuffled through the open door into *Saburo's*. He looked around. With the mass of men seated or standing around, it was hard to pick out Sykes if he was here. Cowell half-hoped Sykes was not there.

However, Cowell spotted his old table near the window, only it now had a full glass of water on top of it. Puzzled, Cowell walked over to it. Did the establishment now place waters on the tables before the patrons sat down?

No sooner had Cowell sat down and scooted his legs under the table than a familiar face showed up. "Hey there." Sykes strolled by with a big smile. "I knew you'd show up again. Doing alright?"

Cowell looked away and tried paying full attention to his glass. "I'm fine."

"Well, I'm sure it rattled you a little bit." Sykes sat opposite Cowell.

Cowell grimaced. "You heard about the gunman, the thief they shot and killed?"

"Word gets around quickly if you have the ear of the right people. I don't have to rely on a phone to get the latest news." Sykes straightened out his shirt. "So, I guess you decided to take me up on my offer?"

Cowell drank heavily as Sykes spoke. With a wipe of his mouth, Cowell said, "If you can get me safely to Fall Crossing, then I'm in."

"Good. I trust you found out where Doc Sam keeps his gasoline?" Sykes said.

"Yeah. It's locked up in his garage."

Sykes nodded. “Not a bad place to keep it.” He reached down and dug out something small from his right jeans pocket. “I thought you might need to get through a locked door.” He slapped the object onto the table, but kept it hidden underneath his hand. “Use these babies. They’ll pick padlocks, deadbolts, knob locks, anything that Doc Sam will use.”

Sykes lifted his hand. The man had produced three metal picks of varying sizes. Cowell took another swig as he looked at the tools and realized what Sykes wanted him to do. Then Cowell said, “I’ve, uh, never picked a lock before.”

Sykes grinned. “That’s alright. I know you’re a greenhorn.” He reached into his other pocket and pulled out a padlock. “We got a little time to practice.”

CHAPTER SIXTEEN

JACOB BROUGHT his bike to a halt. With a curve to the right, Road 212 led right into the small town of Middleburg. It was not a moment too soon. The sky above was starting to dim. Night was approaching.

He wiped sweat from his brow. "Thank God." His relief turned to mild surprise. Should the road just outside of Middleburg be this quiet?

The big shutdown only happened two days ago. Most of the town still should be here. If they wanted to leave, they would have prepared for a long journey. Even with two days, a lot of people might not have finished packing. Hell, they might not even know where to go.

He inhaled the soft blowing air. It didn't feel hot to his nostrils. He was checking for smoke, for signs of a fire. The lack of running water would increase the fire risk. Added to that, a riot or a mob also could burn buildings and cars. The lack of smoke encouraged him. Perhaps this town had held it together.

He pedaled a little farther toward the town boundary. Road 212 spiked through the center of Middleburg. Multiple streets forked off to run through the town.

Where is everybody?

Jacob's journey turned up constant serenity that was beginning to make him nervous. As expected, all of the streetlights and building lights were out, and the streets were free of motorists. But nobody was out and about either, no one to come and tell Jacob about the state of the town.

Or what if snipers are hiding around corners or up on roofs? Fresh sweat poured down Jacob's face. He was getting paranoid. The dusk was not helping. If he wanted to spend the night in the forest, he would have to turn around now to take advantage of the remaining sunlight for travel.

But I can reach Doctor Nguyen?! Middleburg isn't very big. C'mon, what was that street again?

Jacob fished out the instructions Doc Sam had given him. Whitmore Street. It wasn't far. He'd have to find Ballenger Road, which forked off from Road 212. He could make it, but he'd have to put the pedal to the medal.

THE ADDRESS LED Jacob to a loft, accessible by an outside stairwell that ran up the side of the building. This must be Doctor Nguyen's home. Jacob had expected Nguyen's office would be inside an office building where it could be accessed by an elevator. This location appeared to be a small housing complex. Not the kind of place for a doctor to receive patients.

Your daughter just was treated inside a house made of sandbags, he reminded himself. He chuckled. Perhaps he shouldn't be surprised at what he might discover.

He parked the bike underneath the stairs before traversing the steps up to the door above. Then he pushed the doorbell.

Jacob cringed. "Damn." *The power's out, you dumbass*. This still was taking a lot of getting used to.

He gently tapped on the door. Jacob figured he should identify himself as well. In this environment, a knock at thc door could scnd somconc into conniptions.

"Doctor Nguyen! Doctor Sam sent me, from Trapp!"

Jacob waited a minute, but he received no response. Perhaps Doctor Nguyen did not trust that Jacob was telling the truth. Doc Sam had warned that Nguyen might not buy Jacob's story right off the bat. Fortunately, Doc Sam provided some proof to help convince Doctor Nguyen.

Jacob reached into his pocket and pulled out a photograph. Then he held it up to the door's peephole. "Doctor Nguyen! Doc Sam gave this to me! He said you would recognize it!" Doc Sam had provided this aged photograph to Jacob with the belief that Doctor Nguyen would not believe that anyone but someone who had met with Doc Sam could produce it.

But even after another minute's wait, Jacob was left with no reply. Was Doctor Nguyen even home?

Jacob patted the pouch on his left pant leg. This would be his last resort. Doc Sam told him if he received no response from Nguyen, then he should let himself in anyway. Jacob pulled out a brass key. It fit the front door's lock perfectly.

Doc, just tell him he's not going to blow my ass away if I open his door.

He pushed open the door.

To his relief, no gunshots greeted him. In fact, nothing presented itself but the darkness of an unlit living room.

"Doctor Nguyen!" Jacob cried out. "I mean you no harm! Doc Sam sent me!" Jacob waved the photo around, although it was unlikely Nguyen would be able to see it in this darkness. Only an uncovered window provided any light, and with the sun setting, soon this living room would lose that small amount of light.

Even though he wasn't sure Doctor Nguyen wasn't hiding somewhere, looking to ambush him as a possible intruder, Jacob decided he had to search the place more thoroughly. The first place he approached at the end of the living room was a door to the kitchen. After pushing it open, he slowly inched inside. The kitchen was still. No Doctor Nguyen, no anybody.

Jacob's search took him down a small hall to a bedroom and a bathroom, both devoid of human life. It was clear now that Doctor Nguyen was not home. Jacob had looked everywhere he could think of, including in the bedroom closet, for where the doctor might be hiding.

His apprehension was turning to bitter disappointment. What did Doctor Nguyen's absence mean? The apartment did not look disturbed, so it was not as if intruders had shown up and kidnapped him. Jacob shivered. Entertaining such dark possibilities disturbed him. Yet he had to consider all options.

Jacob next considered that the doctor might have left a note, but then he realized that Nguyen lived alone. Doc Sam had mentioned his friend had no wife and that his eldest son lived in Washington state, so he had no reason to leave a clue to his present whereabouts.

Or, he simply could have stepped out to find something to eat.

Jacob laughed as he recognized the simplest explanation might be the best one. What if the doctor simply was out and was coming back? Jacob then winced. What would Doctor Nguyen do if he found his home broken into and Jacob waiting inside? If Nguyen was armed, Jacob could end up as a bloody splatter on the carpet before he could explain why he was here.

I wish I could stay. It's getting dark out. However, meeting Doctor Nguyen here could be counterproductive and, at worst, disastrous. He wasn't an invited guest. Better to leave.

As he stepped out of the front door, he remembered Doc Sam had advised him what to do if Doctor Nguyen wasn't home. He had options. Once he got downstairs, all he had to do was...

He had to hold that thought. Someone was coming.

A tall man was strolling toward the bottom of the stairwell. Instantly, Jacob could tell he wasn't Doctor Nguyen, who was of Vietnamese descent and, at least in the photograph Doc Sam had given him, had short dark hair. This man had long blonde hair and was very tall. Also, judging from his rumpled bulky jacket, he probably was bulked up.

Shit. Jacob could not climb down the stairs without running into this stranger. What would happen? Was this man coming up to call on Doctor Nguyen? Or perhaps this man had something else in mind?

Almost on instinct, Jacob fled back into the apartment and closed the door. After locking it, he raced through the living room to the hall, trying to keep away from windows. Then, Jacob huddled on the other side of the doorframe and waited.

Footsteps approached the door. They grew louder and louder until they crunched on the welcome mat. Then, they stopped. A few seconds later, Jacob overheard something being fed into the lock. This man had a key!

What the hell? Did this man share an apartment with Doctor Nguyen? Again, Doc Sam had been clear that Nguyen lived alone.

Jacob fled into Nguyen's bedroom and closed the door before the mystery man could open the front door. His breathing accelerated as he looked for a place to hide. No, he shouldn't hide. He should try escaping. If he hid somewhere, he would be cornered.

He turned to the window. The glass pane could be slid upward, and at its current width, would permit Jacob to crawl out onto a fire escape beyond. But would he have time to open it?

Thinking fast, Jacob grabbed a chair and shoved it under the door's knob. He would have to buy some time in case this didn't work as quickly as he had hoped. He located two latches on the window frame. He turned the one on the left with no trouble. The right, however, was a different story. It swiveled slightly, before jamming.

Footsteps approached from down the hall. The man was coming. *Damn this thing, open!*

He pushed so hard that a jolt of pain ran through his hand, but he ignored it. Indeed, the pain was worth it, for that extra effort had turned the latch all the way open. Now Jacob was able to push up on the window.

The bedroom knob turned, or rather, tried to.

"Hey!" The voice on the other side was gruff. "What the hell?" The knob rattled harder.

Jacob put all of his strength into raising the window. It was not easy, since the window dragged, perhaps due to not being opened in a long time.

As Jacob finally hoisted the window to its full height, the man on the other side of the door became irate. "Hey! Is somebody in there?"

Jacob ducked down and sped onto the fire escape. He thought about closing the window back down to prevent the intruder from pursuing him easily, but right now all he cared about was putting distance between himself and this damned apartment.

So, he climbed down the steps. He was in such a hurry that his foot slipped, and he had to grasp the bars that held the steps for support. He was in fine shape, but he was not a Hollywood stuntman. One wrong move and he might topple down the steps or even fall off completely.

Finally, his boots slammed down on the hard surface of the sidewalk that ran by the apartment building. Jacob quickly took off straight ahead. He didn't stop to take stock of his surroundings. Distance was all that mattered. He would widen the gap between himself and this invader by any means possible.

He heard the intruder hit the sidewalk behind him. It sounded pretty far away. Had Jacob eluded him?

"Hey! Where the hell did you go, you little maggot?" the man shouted.

A new stairwell loomed ahead. It was situated near a brick outcropping from another apartment building. Jacob decided getting off the street was the better move, and so he turned and ducked under the stairwell.

From here, he could see out into the street. The blond man pursuing him was jogging in the middle of the street, turning his head in different directions. He wasn't running directly toward Jacob's position. So, the intruder in Doctor Nguyen's apartment had not spotted him after all.

But then, Jacob spotted movement from the other side of the street. A second man approached the intruder. He was much shorter than the home invader, with a bald head, a baggy jacket and ripped jeans. Jacob listened as the two men spoke.

"What happened?" asked the short man.

"Beats the hell out of me," said the tall blond man, "Somebody was in there and I chased him off. I didn't get a good look at the son of a bitch."

"He broke in?" the short man asked.

"I don't see how, unless he picked the damn front door. I didn't see any signs that he broke in through a window" the blond man replied.

"Did he take anything?" the short man asked.

"Didn't look like it. He barricaded himself in the bedroom, so I guess I caught him by surprise. If he grabbed anything, it wasn't very big. Maybe he fished through a drawer or something."

The short man laughed at his companion's reply. "Yeah, maybe he stole some money. Good luck trying to use that! So, what do you want to do?"

"The big man isn't going to like the idea of thieves running around. We should do a little patrolling. If we catch him, it's his ass," the blond man said.

"Can't take too long. They want us to report in soon," the short man said.

Jacob was baffled. Who were these men? Were they part of a criminal gang? And who was the "big man" they spoke of?

The pair did not depart the street upon ending their talk. They spread out, with the blond man taking the left side and the short man patrolling the right. They were searching for him.

Jacob couldn't stay. If they crossed past where he was hiding, they might spot him, or at the least, cut off his route of escape. If they possessed guns and were good shooters, they possibly could nail him in the back as he ran. But if he retreated now, those two would not have a straight line to catch him. They would have to arc around until they got behind him, which would be precious seconds for Jacob to try eluding them.

And so, as soon as the blond man's back was turned, Jacob fled.

CHAPTER SEVENTEEN

JACOB WISHED he could shut himself up, but his lungs continued to gulp in large amounts of fresh air. Lying here in this dark corner next to a garbage dumpster was the only place he felt safe enough to rest.

Did I lose him? God, please tell me I did. He was sure he had heard one or maybe both of the men pursue him. Yet, he could not bring himself to stand up and look around the corner to confirm his fears. Besides, he did not want to encounter trouble without rebuilding some of his stamina.

How did this happen? No Doctor Nguyen, no medical supplies. All he had got for his trouble was a dark apartment and pursuit from a possible assailant? He wanted to cuss into the sky except he thought someone might hear him.

Once he finally had his breathing under control, he started thinking a little clearer. Okay, Doctor

Nguyen was not home. Doc Sam thought this might happen. Perhaps Doctor Nguyen had gone to his office instead. Doc Sam warned Jacob to be careful if he tried going there. There could be a rush on Nguyen's office and medical clinics in general from people looking for supplies or treatment if they were injured due to the EMP. Jacob might arrive there only to find an inhospitable crowd.

Still, he could not leave Middleburg empty-handed. He had to check out Nguyen's office.

JACOB'S HEART sank the moment he stepped through the open glass door. He finally reached the building to Doctor Nguyen's clinic. All of the adjoining doors in the hall, the ones that led to other offices, lay open. There was no receptionist in the clinic building's lobby. Dirty shoeprints streamed out of the doors. People had been here, and they may have looted the place.

So far, Jacob's trip here had been uneventful. After his quick getaway, he had doubled back to his bike, finding it, to his relief, still where he had left it. Then he had followed Doc Sam's instructions to reach this building. Doctor Nguyen's office was on the first floor, down the hallway. Jacob had cased the building as best he could before entering. To his relief, the place had not been looted. However, there also was nobody here. Jacob did not know what that meant. What would keep the people of Middleburg away from a medical facility during an emergency?

Jacob proceeded, slowly. There still was some light shining through the windows, but it would not last for much longer.

He peered into the first office. The room was still. Jacob identified an examination table for a patient to sit on, a chair on wheels, a diagram of the inside of a human head, and a wall clock that was stopped. Anything else had been taken.

An examination of a second office told a similar story. No doubt about it. This place had been stripped clean.

Still, he could not leave until he had checked out Doctor Nguyen's office. It was close by. He had to see if anything was left in there.

At first glance, Jacob's fears were confirmed. The place had been stripped clean. No antibiotics. No iodine. No bandages. No anesthetic gas.

As he leaned against an examination table to sigh, he heard a shuffling sound, probably a mouse. With these open doors, it would be easy for a critter to roam about inside the offices. But then Jacob thought he heard an accompanying breath. A human being must be nearby.

Jacob checked around the office. By now the light was very faint, so it was possible he could have missed something or someone in here. He felt along the walls. Maybe there was another door around here, a door that led somewhere else.

His hand brushed against a doorframe. *Damn. I can't believe I missed this.* The door wasn't very wide, though, and in this darkness it almost blended into the scenery perfectly. He felt around until he grasped a doorknob. He pulled it open.

A small woman sat on the floor, drawing her knees against her chest, huddled in the corner of the closet. If Jacob was not aware that someone was in here, he might have missed her.

"Hey," Jacob said, calmly, "are you okay? Don't worry, I'm not here to hurt anyone."

The woman raised her head, enough for her eyes to see up above her knees. Jacob held his palms open to show he was not carrying a weapon. "See?" he asked, "no one else is with me."

The woman did not seem convinced. Jacob wondered if his tattoos might not be giving the best first impression. He figured he should try engaging her. "I'm looking for the doctor of this office. His name is Doctor Nguyen. Do you know where he is?"

Jacob received no answer. Perhaps she feared what he might do to her. He had to prove his good intentions. "A friend of his told me to go find him. Doctor Samuel of Trapp. Doc Sam said that Doctor Nguyen has supplies that he will give me. Doc Sam, he helped my daughter. I have to repay him for the supplies he used."

The woman tilted her head a little higher, revealing her nose. "What...happened?"

"My daughter was hit in the arm by a stray arrow. A hunter trespassed on my property and was shooting off arrows."

"Is she okay?"

"Doctor Sam performed surgery on her, took out the arrow. He believes she'll be fine. She's resting at his place with my family."

"How old is she?"

"She's going to be sixteen soon." Jacob smiled. "We were planning her party just before all this hit."

The woman sat up higher, allowing her face to be fully exposed. "What's your name?" she asked.

"Jacob Avery," he replied.

"I'm Rosc Chcn." She finally stood up, rcvcaling hcr small, thin frame to Jacob. Jacob backed up, so she could walk out of the closet. She still strode gingerly, as if she expected someone to pop out from the darkness at any moment.

"You were hiding," Jacob said. "What happened here?"

"I came to see Doctor Nguyen." Rose coughed. The air in this office was dry and a little warm. The open doors, thankfully, provided some circulation.

"He wasn't here. Then the men came. I heard screaming, so I ran in here and hid in the closet. They came and took..." She pointed to the office. "... everything. I heard it. I heard their voices."

"Do you know who they were? I mean, were they a gang, a mob?" Jacob asked.

"One of the men said he was from the mayor's office and it was by order of the mayor," Rose replied. "Everything here was to be taken to city hall."

"The mayor's office." Jacob scratched the side of his head. "The mayor wanted all this stuff confiscated? Why?"

"I don't know. I just know what I heard."

Jacob shook his head. This made no sense. Why move all the medical supplies out of this clinic? Was it for security purposes? If so, why couldn't the mayor send police here to provide protection? Was this building at risk for some reason?

"Were there any riots outside?" Jacob asked. "Anything that would put this place in danger?"

"There was some commotion. I heard shouting outside, and probably someone was shot." Rose crossed her arms over her chest. "Then I heard someone say the mayor had declared a curfew and that he was sending out a new civilian patrol force."

"A curfew, huh?" Well, that made some sense to Jacob. He also figured a town mayor would reach out to the populace for additional help in maintaining law and order. But Rose clearly did not trust them. Why else would she duck in here? And wouldn't the mayor post some police here to tell anyone who came by what was going on?

Jacob leaned against the patient table again. "It's so damn odd." Returning his gaze to Rose, he added,

"I don't know what your mayor is up to, but I think we should be a little careful about this. Do you live close by?"

"Yes," Rose replied.

"Do you have family here, too?" Jacob asked.

"No. My parents live in Sideburg."

"That's not too far away. Maybe you can make a run for it in the morning. Go home, hunker down, and then peel out when dawn comes."

Rose trembled. "I-I think I could try that. I just... I just don't know what is happening to us."

Jacob sighed. Rose likely didn't even understand that an EMP had struck. He wished he could do more for her, but time was of the essence. He now was down two options. If he was going to find the supplies Doc Sam wanted, he was going to have to pick someplace that had not been cleaned out yet.

SITTING in the kitchen by the dining table, Cowell zipped up his get home bag. His last inspection confirmed that Moses Travers had stocked the bag with everything that he had promised.

But I can't take this with me, he thought. *I'll need to move quickly. If I go through with this, it just will weigh me down.*

A familiar shadow crossed the threshold. Domino peeked in. "Hey," she said.

Cowell sat up and tried to look dignified. "I trust you're doing alright after what just happened?"

"Not too bad." Domino strolled a little way into the room. "I think we're all just glad it's over. He won't be harming anyone ever again. What about you? You were pretty close to it."

"It's not what I expected for my afternoon, but I will manage. I suppose I'll just have to get used to occurrences such as these."

"I wish you didn't have to go to Fall Crossing alone. Are you sure you don't want to wait here for a few days, maybe find someone to escort you or find a traveling party? Doctor Sam said pretty soon people might start traveling in packs for security. One of them might head south toward Richmond. They could drop you off in Fall Crossing."

Cowell clasped his hands together. "Tempting, but I think I'd like to end my nightmare as soon as possible. I know I'll be safe once I reach my sister."

"Are you and your sister okay? Are you sure she'll take you in? You didn't sound like you were on great terms."

"I'd say our terms are...adequate. I'm sure she won't turn me away with what's going on. An emergency has a funny way of reordering your priorities."

"No kidding." Domino leaned against the doorframe. "I guess you've been thinking about that, about your priorities?"

Cowell sighed. "I've thought about nothing else.

It's been eating at me, actually. You might be shocked to hear this, but now I actually envy you."

Domino laughed. "Really?"

"This is the world you were born for. What you prepared for, what you trained for. This is not my world anymore. I don't understand it and I fear I will not survive in it."

"I'm sure this all has knocked you for a loop. That's why you should stay and not run off by yourself. You could learn how to take care of yourself. There are people here who would teach you, in exchange for some help." She exhaled softly. "I'm sure even Jay wouldn't mind giving you a few pointers."

Cowell chuckled under his breath. "Your husband is not a great fan of mine. I think you presume too much of his kindness."

"Hey, I'm the one who's married to him." Domino laughed again. "You might be surprised. If you give him a reason, I think he could overlook a lot of what happened between you and our family."

Cowell looked into Domino's eyes. "You think that could happen?"

"I know it," she replied.

Cowell scratched his chin. "It's a very tempting offer. Thank you. I'll give it some thought."

Domino eventually left to check on Jubilee, leaving Cowell once again to ponder his imminent course of action.

So far, so good.

Jacob thought the pharmacy down the street was his best bet. From here, Jacob could discern a few promising signs, not the least of which was that the place had not been ransacked. The glass windows and doors were not broken, and debris did not clutter the front of the establishment. There were also no people around, no angry rioters, but also no policemen either. Jacob might have been disturbed earlier by the lack of the latter, but after hearing Rose's story, he wasn't sure about the lawmen of this town either.

He bristled upon remembering her. Regrettably, he had had to part ways with her, but she seemed okay with the idea of making it home. At least she had a goal to reach. Hopefully, she could escape Middleburg tomorrow and find her family.

Jacob took one last look down the street. Finding it still empty, he decided to make his move. He would leave his bike here and then trek down to the pharmacy. He didn't want to leave it too close to the pharmacy. Even though having quick access to the bike might be a smart move, he still had to mount it and start pedaling, and that actually would eat up time if he was being pursued. In case he ran into those men from Nguyen's apartment or some other unsavory character, he wanted to stay on foot. He always could loop around to pick up the bicycle later.

He crossed the road quickly, leaving his bicycle on the other side. The dark shadows cast by the store awnings helped provide his vehicle with some shielding. The continuing nightfall would do the rest.

Even if he made it inside, he still couldn't be sure he would find everything on Doc Sam's list. In fact, he was sure he couldn't, at least not any anesthetic gas. However, Doc Sam had sounded understanding about his chances and offered him the option to bring back items comparable to those on his list. If he couldn't secure anesthetic gas, he could try locating some lidocaine.

"And if I come up too short, what then?" Middleburg was not very big. He might not be able to find a facility that possessed what he was looking for. Pleasantville was his closest fallback choice but going there only increased the risk factor too high for Jacob to feel comfortable.

He reached the glass doors. He stopped in front of them, half-expecting them to slide open, but he rapidly recalled the dearth of power. At least he was remembering more quickly that the country's electronics were out.

Damn, I'm actually getting used to this.

He pressed his hand against the door. It would not budge. He pushed a little harder with the same result. Was the door really locked in place when not in use? Or was it manually locked?

There's one way to find out.

Jacob scoped out the front windows. Soon he discovered what he was looking for—a white sign that was flipped to the "closed" side. These people locked up, perhaps when they realized their store was at risk.

I wonder why the mayor hasn't cleared out this place? There's a lot of supplies inside. Or maybe they just hadn't come here yet. By "yet," Jacob implied to himself that this location might be next on the list. He would have to move quickly.

CHAPTER EIGHTEEN

Cowell eyed the garage door. It was now or never. *Damn. I can't believe I'm doing this.* But sheer necessity demanded it. He was not a survivor, not like the Averys. He admitted that to himself. Anything else would be a lie, and Alex Cowell vowed if anything else, he would not deceive himself.

He pulled out the lock pick. If Sykes' instructions were on the mark, it would not take much to unlock the hanging lock that bound the garage door through a hole in a small swinging panel.

So, Cowell slipped the pick into the keyhole and turned it. He kept as silent as he could, waiting for the telltale click that told Cowell he had completed his task.

Fresh sweat poured down his face. He didn't like this. What if Doc Sam spotted him? Would the doctor shoot him on the spot for theft? Even when the lights were on, when society was still fully functioning, a property owner had broad prerogative to deal with an invader without punishment. Who was going to restrain Doc Sam now?

Focus. Stop sweating it out.

No. I should throw in the towel. This isn't going to work. It...

The lock clicked. It was loose. A simple yank was all it took to pull the lock's tongs loose.

That was one lock. Now for the deadbolt.

Cowell fished out the pick Sykes had told him to use for this task. With a little more confidence, he unlocked this lock, and in a shorter period of time.

The third lock, the one in the knob itself, awaited. Cowell gave Doc Sam credit; the man did not skimp on locking up his garage.

You still can stop this. Relocking these locks would not be hard. Surely no one has seen you. Doctor Samuel and Domino Avery won't be the wiser.

He stuck the same pick into the knob lock. No, he was too committed to this. He had to carry through. Besides, he would not see the Averys or the doctor again after this. He likely never would come by this way again. They would not give him much thought except to nurse whatever resentments arose from his burglary.

The lock turned. He had done it! A slight twist of the knob later, and he was inside the garage. He shut the door slowly. He could not allow the door to hang open, even if the garage was very hot inside.

Cowell checked around for the gasoline tanks.

They likely would be conspicuous. If Doc Sam had stored a large amount of gasoline, it had to be held in tanks, perhaps handheld portable tanks.

He might have hidden them, he thought. Cowell wouldn't put it past the eccentric doctor to think that intruders might penetrate his garage and find the fuel. What if Doctor Samuel had placed the fuel in a container with a different label? For all Cowell knew, the doctor could have the fuel in a tank marked "fertilizer."

"Or maybe the simplest solution is the best one," he whispered. With all the stuff in this garage, perhaps it was just hard to find anything in here.

DOMINO STUCK her head into Doc Sam's bedroom. The doctor had given them permission to go inside if he wasn't around. Interestingly, there was very little inside it anyway, just his bed and nightstand, plus a closed closet door, and a soft chair near the window. Her son was hanging off the chair, his eyes glued to a set of binoculars. He was staring out the back window.

"Now what are you up to?" she asked with a laugh. "Careful, you might fall off."

"Just looking out to the road," Brandon replied, "looking out for cyborgs."

Domino took hold of Brandon and pulled him

back onto the chair's main seat. "So you are. Seen anything we should worry about?"

Brandon took off his binoculars. "Naaah. I just see people walking around, but not lately. I think because it's getting dark soon."

"I can understand that." Domino shivered a little. "It's so strange to be in a town with no lights."

Brandon shifted so he was more firmly anchored to the chair. Then he took another look through the binoculars. "Hey, that's weird. That truck wasn't there before."

"What do you mean?" Domino knelt down beside him.

"That delivery truck." Brandon pointed to the right. "It was all the way over there. Now it's right there in that intersection." He leaned off the edge of the chair. "It's moving!"

"Easy." Domino caught Brandon before he fell off. "What do you mean it's moving? Someone's driving it?"

"No, it's just rolling." Yeah, I see it! It's rolling!"

"Let me see." Domino took the binoculars and placed them against her face.

"It's almost out of sight, but yeah, it's moving. I don't think it's actually on. I see them! There's a man. He's pushing it from behind." She tried extending the focus. "I think there's someone else. Two men, probably just pushing that truck. It's gone now." She handed the binoculars back to Brandon.

"What was the deal?" Brandon asked.

"They probably released the parking brake and are moving it someplace out of the way," Domino said.

"But why did they push it down the street? There's a parking lot all the way to the right. I saw it yesterday." Brandon narrowed his eyes. "Unless they are cyborgs!"

Domino wanted to chuckle, but something about Brandon's comment did puzzle her. Who would go through that much trouble to move a large truck like that? "That street does hit an intersection with the street just outside this house."

"You think they're trouble?" Brandon asked.

Domino shook her head. "A couple of guys pushing a delivery truck? Probably not." She couldn't shake a weird feeling about it, though.

"Brandon, stay inside and look after your sister until I come back." Domino turned toward the hall.

COWELL HUFFED. The stifling air in this damn garage was getting to him. His shirt and pants were sticky with sweat. Yet, his search had turned up nothing so far. He had to push aside heavy equipment and tools just to clear away walls and wall corners in the hope the tanks would be there.

"He said he has gas. So, where the hell is it?" Cowell then clamped his mouth shut. What if somebody on the outside heard him?

He leaned against the back side of the truck. "Think! Think!" Doctor Samuel had to have hidden the tanks somewhere, but Cowell was running out of places to look. Cowell even had looked inside the truck itself to see if the doctor had secreted the fuel behind the back seat or under the tarp that concealed the truck bed, but to no avail.

Still huffing, Cowell stood up. He had to have missed something. He had checked the truck, the areas by the walls, near the workbench...

The workbench!

Cowell rushed to the bench, nearly tripping over a few tools in the process. He had looked to the sides of the bench, but not underneath it! With the dim light and the large wooden posts, it was not easy to see underneath it. Cowell squatted down and peered beneath. The darkness made it difficult, but Cowell would not be deterred. He leaned in closer, almost poking his head under the bench frame. He reached inside. His fingers grazed a solid surface.

That might be it! Cowell backed off and looked directly where he had touched something. A solid box lay against the wall. With a laugh, he grabbed the box and dragged it out. Cowell had unearthed a cardboard box.

He yanked open the lid. A red gasoline tank lay inside, full. So, Cowell's suspicions were correct. The doctor had hidden away some gas in a place where it would not be discovered easily.

Cowell knelt down and searched beneath the

bench again. He soon discovered a second box with a second gas tank.

"I did it." Cowell repeated, over and over, before finishing with, "I can't believe I outfoxed that crazy doctor."

Now to take these two cans and hurry back to Sykes. He was as good as gone from this town!

———

"It doesn't sound like anything to be worried about," Doc Sam said as Domino marched through the living room up to the front window. "Trevor Smith rounded up five men to push some cars off Waldo Street yesterday. Wanted to clear the road. Sounds as though Trevor and his crew might be doing the same to that delivery truck you saw."

"You're probably right." Domino looked at the darkening sky. "I guess I'd feel better if it wasn't so close to nighttime." She returned her attention to the doctor. "Can I just take a look outside? I just want some peace of mind."

"I learned never to say no to a lady with a gun." Doc Sam chuckled. "Go ahead. If you like, I'll keep an eye on you from a few paces."

———

Cowell planted the two cans on the dirt. "Damn."

He was exhausted. His body cried out for rest. The search inside that hot garage had sapped him.

He flung sweat off his face. “No. Got to...got to get the hell out of here.”

After taking the cans back in hand, he shuffled past the side of the garage. However, once he reached the other side, he stopped and leaned against the garage’s rear. No matter what he thought, he was not physically strong enough to endure long work in the heat. But at least since this part of the garage did not face Doctor Samuel’s house, he would not be noticed if he rested here.

His breathing slowed. He was starting to get his bearings. Another few minutes, and he would be strong enough to walk toward the street. His ordeal was soon to end.

However, the sound of a female voice cut through his euphoria. Domino was outside! Cowell also overheard crunching footsteps. She was walking in his direction.

DOMINO KEPT her attention on the street as she walked toward it. So far, she had not spotted any sign of the delivery truck. Then again, if the truck had not made the turn down this street, Domino would not spot it unless she stepped in the middle of the road and looked to the intersection. And even if she had, the truck might be gone if the men had kept pushing it.

She shook her head. Fine. She'd walk into the street and look, but if she saw nothing, she was returning inside and shaking off the whole thing.

However, something else caught her attention.

Doc Sam's garage mostly had filled her field of vision, but she had been looking away from it to the street. However, she could not ignore the fact that the door was slightly open. The padlock was gone. Someone had gone into the garage.

But Doc Sam and Brandon are inside the house, and Jubilee is resting. A cold jolt ran down her spine. *Who else could it be? Cowell? Isn't he inside, too? And besides, the garage usually is locked up. Doc Sam has to be on hand to unlock it. Did Doc Sam unlock it for him?*

"Cowell!" Domino cried out, "Cowell, are you there?"

Shit! Shit! Shit! What the hell do I do?

Domino was calling for him. She knew he was out here. Cowell remembered that he had left the garage door open. He had figured he was as good as gone, so why relock it? Thanks to his stupidity, Domino had been tipped off.

"Cowell?" Domino called from the other side of the garage, "Hey! Are you in there or what?"

Calm down, Cowell thought. *She doesn't know you*

did anything. Maybe if you go out there and talk to her, you can get her to go back inside. Leave the gas here. She won't see it. Go back for it later.

It seemed like a good plan. There was no way he could flee with the gas in hand now. She would spot him and catch up to him for sure. A good bluff was his only chance.

DOMINO'S JAW TIGHTENED. No one was responding from the garage. She would have to run back and ask Doc Sam if he had let anyone inside. If not, they had an intruder on their hands.

But before Domino could flee back to the house, Cowell ran from the other side of the garage. "Miss Avery! I heard your voice! Is everything alright?"

"Cowell!" Domino exhaled deeply. "Damn! I thought for a moment we had trouble." Cowell stopped a few steps short of the garage, leaving a wide gap between them. "Doc Sam. He let you inside, didn't he? Why?"

"Oh, the garage." Cowell pointed to the building behind him. "Yes. Yes, he did. The good doctor was very neighborly. He let me, uh, that is, add some tinder to my backpack, for the trip to Fall Crossing. He kept it in there."

Boy, he's nervous about something. I've never seen Cowell that flustered, not even when we were talking about the EMP. "Well, want me to help you? It's getting dark and we shouldn't be out here."

"Actually, I'm finished. I should lock up. My apologies. I left the door open."

Domino frowned. *For such a by the book guy, he sure is sloppy today*.

"You can go on ahead. I'll finish up here," Cowell said.

Domino nodded. "Okay." She turned to walk back to the house, but something bugged her. Didn't Doc Sam and Moses Travers give Cowell some tinder? Why would he need more of it?

Well, I suppose some more tinder certainly wouldn't hurt at all. In fact, he might need some for a few days' trip. Even so, she couldn't quell her discontent until she heard from the man himself.

"Hey! Doc Sam!" Domino cried toward the front door. "Did you let Alex Cowell into the garage?"

Cowell's eyes widened. At the same time Doc Sam pushed open the front door. "Did I let who into the garage?"

Domino felt her question mostly had been answered already. Cowell looked shocked, as if he had been caught in bed with someone else's spouse.

But before Doc Sam could supply a full answer, the sound of a roaring truck engine cut through the air. Domino turned to the street. The delivery truck that Brandon had spotted was barreling down the street—with the ignition running. The truck sped past the house and stopped on the other side of the garage.

Two men ran into the open. "Hey! Move it!"

Cowell turned and fled behind the garage. Domino started running after him. The rear of the garage soon became visible to Domino, allowing her to see two more men grabbing gasoline tanks off the ground.

"Cowell! What the hell is going on?" Domino cried out.

Cowell turned and flashed her a look of shock, anguish, perhaps even regret. But the two men reached him and grabbed him by the shoulders. "Come on, let's go!" one of them shouted.

"Cowell!" Domino drew her gun. She wasn't sure exactly what was happening, but she deduced those gas tanks were not theirs. They must have come from the garage. Cowell was stealing Doc Sam's gasoline!

Cowell was being ushered around the front of the truck. At the same time, one of the men whipped out a pistol. Domino jumped to the ground. Shots rang out, but all of them either struck the side of the garage or the ground close by her.

Domino bit her lip so hard it was bleeding. The gunfire had stopped. Domino clung to the shadow of the garage wall as she inched forward, looking to see if she could return fire. But instead she heard the delivery truck kick into drive and pull away from Doc Sam's property.

CHAPTER NINETEEN

"DOMINO!" Doc Sam charged up to her with a loaded gun in his hands. "Did they hit you? Are you alright?"

Domino climbed to her feet. "I'm fine." She wiped a bit of blood off her lip. "Bastards. Goddamn bastards!" She kicked a pebble into the street, right where the delivery truck had stopped. Domino then coughed. The exhaust from the truck still was fresh.

"I saw them take something," Doc Sam said.

"Tanks. Looked like gas tanks." Domino brushed dirt off her pant legs. "Cowell must have broken in and took them."

"I hid a supply under the workbench," Doc Sam said. "Must have searched that place, hard to find them."

Domino cringed. "I can't believe it. Why? Who the hell were those guys? Did Cowell know them all along?"

"Calm yourself," Doc Sam said, "you're more upset over it than I am."

"And how's that truck even working?" Domino pointed to the street. "The EMP, didn't it shut down every car and truck on the road?"

"Mrs. Avery!" Doc Sam did not raise his voice much, but it was enough to snap Domino out of her rage, at least enough for her to heed his words.

Domino cringed. "I'm sorry. I'm just..."

"The important thing is that no one was killed. Let's hurry back inside and discuss what happened. I'm sure your son has heard all the commotion and wants to know you are safe."

COWELL, sitting in the front passenger side seat of the truck, clung to the shoulder strap of his seat belt. He knew Sykes's men had come to get him and had ushered him into the delivery truck. He wasn't expecting that, but he was glad for the quick getaway. However...

"You shot at her?" It was barely a question. He was more outraged than anything else.

The truck's cab had a back seat. Sykes was seated there along with one of his men. "Just a little insurance to keep the woman off your back. Didn't look like we hit her. She'll probably be alright."

The callousness in Sykes's tone rattled Cowell. "We're talking about someone's life here."

"Well, I suppose you thought we were going to use the velvet glove for this operation, huh?" Snark laced Sykes's voice. "You got the gas. I just wanted to make sure we received it with no problem, hence our little 'rescue.'"

The driver, a lanky man with a short black beard, giggled. "You liked our little plan, huh?"

Sykes smiled. "We didn't drive up to Doctor Sam's house. A truck with a running motor would get everybody's attention. So, we pushed this baby close to the house and kept watch over you. When the time was right, we moved in." Sykes pointed to the storage compartment behind the truck cab. "We got quite a haul in there. Some of my boys are back there, along for the ride."

Cowell shrank back into his seat a little. He had wound up with some dangerous men. If he had known these people would turn guns on the Avery woman, he never would have gone along with it.

But she's okay, he thought. The events of today would rattle her in the short term, but she would go on living. His job was to make sure he would go on living. Today, he assured that, or so he hoped.

"So, where are we going now?" Cowell asked.

"Fall Crossing!" Sykes leaned up to the back of Cowell's seat. "A deal's a deal, and you fulfilled your end. Just sit back and enjoy the ride." He chuckled.

Cowell looked to the road ahead. He was riding in a vehicle, just as he had back before the EMP had hit. Cool air blew over his sweat-dampened body. At this rate, he would be in Fall Crossing in hours.

Well, I suppose I'll be a survivor after all. Just in my own way.

And as the minutes passed, the guilt over his actions melted away.

BRANDON STUDIED Domino's right leg. Domino had rolled up the pant leg to check for scrapes or cuts. "It's alright," she said.

Brandon was unusually quiet, perhaps because he had heard the gunshots and wasn't sure for a minute if his mother was alive or dead. Domino spared a moment to console her jittery son.

"So, Mister Cowell was a cyborg," Brandon said.

"Mister Cowell is many things," said Doc Sam as he wandered past. "A fool being foremost among them. I'm afraid he has chosen his path very poorly."

"The man's a snake. I knew it from the start," Domino said.

"You knew he was an overzealous social worker. That doesn't immediately point to a gasoline thief," Doc Sam said.

"Oh, he had it in him this whole time. I don't doubt it," Domino replied with bitterness. "And I led him here. He followed us to Trapp. We led him to your door."

"You couldn't have known what he was going to

do. Most likely, Cowell ran into some unsavory characters while repaying his debt to Moses."

"But how come that truck still was running?" Brandon asked.

"It looked as though it had some years on it," Doc Sam replied. "If it lacked the electronics of many vehicles today, it could have survived the EMP unscathed. There will be a few of those out there. I guess whoever owns that machine bribed Cowell into stealing gas for a prolonged journey."

"Prolonged. Guess that means he's going somewhere far," Domino said.

"Probably to Fall Crossing," Doc Sam said.

"Well, I don't care. I hope I never see his face again." Domino pulled her legs up to the sofa.

Doc Sam looked at Domino with sad eyes. "Why don't you use the tub in the bathroom? I drew enough to bathe myself, but you should go ahead and use it. I'll make a fine dinner for all of you."

Domino put her legs down. "Thanks." At least she would end the day on a happier note.

A shiver suddenly coursed through her body. *Jacob. What is he doing now?*

THE GLASS SHATTERED ALL across the pharmacy floor. One good hard blow with a piece of loose concrete taken from the sidewalk smashed the window dead center, permitting an easy path for

Jacob to dash through. Without electricity, there would be no cameras to document his presence or alarms to alert people, and so far, the street behind him remained empty. So, there were no witnesses to see him break in.

The only thing that stopped him from rushing inside was the odd feeling of breaking into a store. Even though he understood his current circumstances, he couldn't shake how strange it was to break and enter a place of business. In the ordinary world he had known, he would be in the back of a police cruiser in handcuffs in the near future.

But this isn't the ordinary world. Go!

Jacob dashed through the broken pane. He passed by the empty cashier's station on his way to the aisles. A quick look at the aisles confirmed that the pharmacy had not been looted. The shelves still were well stocked. The first round of shelves was filled with two-liter bottles of soda.

Soon he reached the end of the aisle. A lane cut across his path on the way to another round of shelves. Jacob stopped in the lane and looked up for the directory signs. The darkness made it almost impossible to make out the letters on the signs. He was still in the food and drink section. He needed to find the bandages and the medications. Hunting for the supplies down every aisle would eat up a lot of time, time which he wasn't sure he possessed.

Hold on. This shouldn't be too hard. It's hard as hell to see, but you still can make out what medicine looks like. It's in bottles and little boxes. Quick looks at the shelves should tell him whether it was worth it to search that particular aisle.

Jacob eliminated three aisles in quick order—their stock was only food. Jacob felt tempted to check the aisles for cans of soup or vegetables, but food was not his problem. His homestead was self-sufficient for him and his family. The medical supplies were everything tonight.

To his amusement, it was harder to tear himself away from the toy aisle. Seeing the array of plastic figurines and crayons made him think of his children, particularly of Jubilee. Sometimes when she had fallen ill, he would buy her a toy to help cheer her up. Even though she was fifteen and had outgrown toys such as the ones before him, the fatherly instinct to cheer up his little girl still took hold. He also felt a little sad as he recognized shopping for toys would become a thing of the past until society got back on its feet—if it ever did.

By the next aisle, he had found what he was looking for. The shelves were filled with medicines of various types. Of course, now he had to read the boxes, which would be a hell of a task. Still, Doc Sam had given him a few brand names to keep in mind. Those names would be prominently displayed on the boxes. Unfortunately, if he didn't find the right brands, he would have to look more closely. A painkiller, for example, might only be available in the generic brand, which would be a little harder to spot.

No need to bitch about it. Jacob opened his bag and pulled out a small empty corded backpack. Ordinarily, he would use this bag for collecting wood or herbs in the forest. Today, though, it would be used for collecting of a different sort.

Jacob identified the boxes of painkiller medication. He took what he thought would fill Doc Sam's needs. Farther down the shelf, he discovered antibiotic ointments. A few of them went into his bag as well.

If he stumbled upon the antibiotic ointment, he hoped the antibiotics were not far away. He was right, he could see the pharmacist's counter at the end of the aisle. After climbing over the counter and breaking a few locked cabinets, he found what he needed.

Holy shit, I think I hit the jackpot.

The shelves were particularly packed in the antibiotic section. They must have received a recent shipment. There were so many for the taking, but Jacob held off. He reminded himself that this pharmacy still serviced the people of Middlesburg. He had to leave as much of it as possible for them, even if he wondered what the leadership of this town was really up to.

With the oral antibiotics in the bag, Jacob climbed over the counter and back into the general pharmacy area. He moved on to look for lidocaine on the shelf just ahead. He needed something to substitute for the anesthetic gas he could not find.

However, the anesthetics were not on this shelf. Fortunately, they were stocked on the next shelf over.

From there, Jacob checked for bandages. It took a search of the next shelf from the anesthetics to find them. Gauze, big bandages and little band-aids went into his bag.

Am I missing anything? He put his corded bag and get home bag on the floor, and then pulled out Doc Sam's paper. Iodine! That's what he was missing.

He frantically checked for it. However, shelf after shelf yielded nothing until he reached the center of the pharmacy and discovered the iodine. A couple of boxes would suffice.

Jacob let out a breath of relief. He had done it! He almost couldn't believe it. The task had been so hard and so elusive. Now he could pay off Doc Sam and return home with his family.

He stood up and looked down the nearest aisle, gazing at the windows beyond. However, this aisle also happened to be the toy aisle. He couldn't resist checking it out once again.

Specifically, he found something that caught his eye. A plastic doll hung off a top prong. The figure was feminine, with big black button-like eyes and a smile made of an inked line. She was dressed in purple boxing trunks, with red boxing gloves over her hands.

This was a "Cutie Bruiser" doll. Cutie Bruiser was a fictional character who at one time was quite popular and even starred in her own short-lived cartoon series. Even though Cutie Bruiser had fallen into some obscurity in the past couple of years, she always had been Jubilee's favorite.

She had to come home with Jacob. He plucked her off the prong.

As he turned to the side, he noted the small plastic cars in their casings. Brandon would like one of these. He fished off a red car.

But as soon as he plucked the car in his hand, he heard the sound of crunching glass. Someone was in here. The newcomer must be stepping over the broken glass Jacob had made when he had smashed into the pharmacy.

Shit! Who could that be? Another "thief" who spotted the smashed window and decided to avail himself of the opportunity of the pharmacy's stock?

The footsteps multiplied. Soft chatter rang out in the air. Jacob froze in place and listened. All of the voices belonged to men.

"What do you think?" asked one of the men.

"Look, somebody chucked a piece of concrete in here," responded a second man.

"He's got one hell of a throwing arm," the first man said.

Now a third man piped up. "There's got to be a looter inside. I'm surprised this place wasn't taken down already."

"The people here are compliant. They knew when the big man threw down the gauntlet not to screw around," said the second man.

"Look, if there's a looter in there, he's not getting away. The patrol's got the front doors and the windows. He comes this way, we got him," the third man said.

"Perfect. Let's go find the shithead. We got enough men," suggested the second man.

Jacob cringed. The mayor's civilian force had this place surrounded. He was trapped!

CHAPTER TWENTY

JACOB'S MIND raced a mile a second. *Okay, think! What would happen if you revealed yourself to these guys? Would they understand that you need these supplies? No, they sound as if they want to make an example of you. I've got to get out of here.*

The footsteps grew louder. Jacob fled to the back of the pharmacy, along the row of refrigerator doors. The men were not in this wing of the store, but they soon would be. Jacob looked for a door, a place that might lead to a back entrance. There was a booth where a pharmacist could fill out prescriptions, but it also was well exposed. The men surely would spot him if he tried ducking behind the booth. If there was an exit on the other side, he might not find it in time.

His hand flopped against one of the refrigerator door handles. He jiggled it. A stale odor wafted through the crack of the door. With the power out, all of the milk and anything perishable was going bad.

Jacob wanted to move away from the door, but then something occurred to him. When the employees stock this pharmacy's refrigerators, they do so from the other side. There must be a room beyond the fridge shelves. And if there was a room, perhaps there was also an entrance out of here!

The footsteps and chatter continued approaching. Jacob had to act fast. Swiftly, he picked out a fridge that contained the fewest number of shelves—just some frozen dinners. After whipping open the door, he pushed hard on the shelves, jostling them a little. Then he kicked furiously. A few slams of his boot broke the shelves loose and opened up a gap big enough for him to fit in.

"Hey, I heard something!" called out one of the men.

Jacob did not stick around. He was in and through in seconds. His handiwork deposited him into a gray room that ordinarily would be refrigerated. It also stunk like hell. Waves of spoiled meat and dairy products assaulted his nostrils.

The door, the door, where's the door out of here?

Jacob ran to the back wall and felt along it. The lack of light made this place a nightmare to find anything. He searched for anything, a door handle, a crease in the wall, a door hinge...

Rapid rumblings from behind the doors broke his concentration. The men had tracked his noise to the refrigerator doors. With the ocean of darkness in here, it was unlikely they could spot him, but one of them was sure to spot the door where he had kicked out the shelves. If they got wise to his move, they would flood this room very soon.

What if I messed up? What if they really do stock this room from inside the store itself? I may have just trapped myself like a rat!

"Where the hell did he go?" Shouted the second man Jacob had heard. They were very close.

"Is he in there?" asked the third man.

"Don't be stupid. How the hell did he get into there?" the second man questioned.

Ignore them. Find the exit. It's your only chance.

He resumed feeling along the wall.

C'mon, c'mon...

His fingers grazed a crack. He ran his hand up and bumped against a door hinge. Found it!

"Look, just open it up and throw that shit aside!" barked the third man Jacob had overheard. "I tell you, I think he's in there."

Jacob grasped the door handle. He turned while praying it wasn't locked.

His hopes were not dashed. A turn was all it took to open the door to the open night air.

He didn't even take the time to case the outside. He simply ran out and shut the door behind him.

The refrigerator room exit had deposited Jacob on the backside of the pharmacy. He stood under a small awning. There was a parking lot before him, empty, likely used for delivery trucks. Nobody was around. The mayor's force had not thought to secure the back end of the pharmacy.

That didn't mean it would be smooth sailing from here, though. There was a street beyond, and a row of homes lay on the other side. Someone might spot him if he tried to cross over.

I've got to try. They're coming through just behind me. They'll find the door and open it any moment.

He sucked in a deep breath. Then, he ran.

DOMINO, feeling exhausted, shuffled down the hall until she stopped near the open door of Doc Sam's bedroom. Cowell's backpack was lying on the floor, nestled against the wall, close to the bed. Looking at it irritated Domino. The pack was solid evidence of Cowell's treachery. It had been an act of kindness that the social worker had spurned for whatever he got from the men who drove that delivery truck. It also was galling that he had left it in Doc Sam's bedroom, of all places. Cowell must have figured the doctor would not spot in there until he had made his getaway.

She knelt down over it. At least the supplies inside could be returned to better use. She would bring this to Doc Sam. Perhaps he would take it to

Moses Travers. At least Moses would receive back his goods.

Before she could pick it up, she spotted a small piece of paper sticking out of one of the zippers. After opening the compartment, she was able to take the paper out. Evidently, Cowell had left this paper intentionally for Domino to find.

She unfolded it. Cowell had written a short message on the yellow notepad page.

Thank you for your assistance through this difficult time. However, as I said, this is not my world. I cannot understand it any more than you could understand mine. So, I will have to find my own little pocket of safety.

I wish you and your family well.

Alexander Cowell

Domino shook her head. It wasn't an apology. Basically, it was a plea for understanding. He had left the bag in here hoping she would find it first.

"Damn it, Cowell." Domino stood up. She was sincere in wanting him to stay here in Trapp, to find help, to develop the skills he would need to survive. Who the hell did he hook up with in town? What did they tell him they could do for him in exchange for the stolen gas?

"Doms, don't give him a second thought." It was time to close his chapter in the life of the Averys. She should spend her time worrying about her family, particularly Jacob. It was late outside. She feared for his safety. Where was he sleeping right now?

JACOB BRUSHED the last few leaves from his face. The bicycle was in sight. No one had disturbed it.

He took a circular path to get back to this spot. After crossing the street, he fled between a set of houses, but was almost blocked by the thick bushes between them. It took some crawling to get underneath them and out onto an open street. Then he had to remember which direction he needed to go. If he took the wrong way, he would be leaving his bike behind, and he desperately needed it to get out of town.

Fortunately, he was right on target. Once he hit the next intersection, he hung a left and clung to the shadows of the buildings to keep from being spotted.

He mounted his bike. His new load weighed on him a little, but not enough to keep him from pedaling. He wouldn't sleep in Middleburg tonight. He had to get out of here. If he could, he would ride back to Trapp. He might be a sleepless wreck when he reached his family, but at least he would be alive. That was all that mattered.

He began his ride up the street.

However, he did not get more than a few paces before the road was suddenly swarmed by a mob. He put on the brakes. *What the hell?*

There had to be at least twenty of them. They had emerged from the other side of the street, from out of the shadows of the line of stores. One of the men stepped up. He was holding a wooden post. Another man used a lighter to spark a small flame on top of it, creating a torch.

"Well, hello." The torch man smiled. "We thought you'd show up sooner or later. We saw your bike and we figured you'd come back for it. That made it much easier than tearing up the pharmacy to find you."

Jacob cleared his throat. "The pharmacy? I-I don't know what you're talking about."

"You can drop the innocent boy act. You were in there." The torch man looked over Jacob's shoulder. "Looks like you got a pretty sweet haul, didn't you?"

Jacob backed up a step. How the hell could he get out of this? He was boxed in on all sides.

One of the men pointed a rifle at him. "Any guns you got, knives, weapons, drop them now and step away."

Jacob tried pleading with these men again. "Listen, I don't know what you want. I'm not here to hurt anyone. My daughter, she..."

A shot of pepper spray struck him from the left, cutting off his plea. He fell to the ground, his face, nose, and lungs on fire.

"Do it!" yelled the torch man.

Someone spiked his arm with a syringe. He was being drugged. In seconds, he lost consciousness.

"EASY, EASY. CAN YOU HEAR ME?"

Jacob stirred. A man was standing over him. Jacob blinked his eyes. It was hard to discern the man's features. He was short, with spiky short black hair that was graying around his ears. He tugged at a slightly oversized white coat as he looked over Jacob. "The fools. They didn't need to give you that sedative."

Jacob groaned. "I feel like I need a whole gallon of coffee."

"I don't think it'll be that bad. Just rest a few minutes. You'll perk up."

Jacob complied. Little by little, he returned to his senses. He soon got a better look at the man before him. He appeared to be of Asian descent, likely middle-aged. He also was tending to a table that contained a slew of medicine boxes.

Could this guy be him? "Doctor Nguyen?"

"In the flesh. I trust Sam sent you."

"Doc Sam! Yeah, he did. How did you know?"

Nguyen held up the photograph Jacob had been carrying of Doc Sam and Nguyen. "They searched you thoroughly. I told them what this meant, and they gave it to me. Judging from the supplies in your bag, Sam must have done something for you, an operation perhaps."

"Not for me. My daughter. She was hurt. An arrow had got lodged in her arm. He took it out. I had to pay back what he used to help her."

"That's Sam." Nguyen strode closer to Jacob. "You must have gone to my home first. I apologize for not being there. I was 'escorted' here." Nguyen frowned. "My office and all of the others were ransacked. The mayor's office ordered the inventory brought here for security purposes."

"Where is here?" Jacob looked around the room.

"The town hall," Nguyen replied. "It's the base of operations for the mayor and his men. When the lights went out, they moved quickly. They imposed a curfew and ordered stores to be emptied out. They made offers to men in the town to help in exchange for food and water. They knew those things were going to be hard to come by."

"You don't sound as though you trust them," Jacob said.

"I've spent too much in the company of bullies and tyrants not to sense them when they're nearby. By the way, your name?"

"Jacob Avery."

No sooner had he finished introducing himself than he heard a knock at the door. "Doctor Nguyen! Is he awake? We hear voices in there."

"He is!" Nguyen shook his head. "They're going to talk to you."

The door opened. Three men poured out. Nguyen quickly stepped aside as if he was avoiding a speeding car. Upon reaching Jacob, they seized him, hauling him to his feet.

"He's going to want to talk to you," one of the men said.

"He?" Jacob asked as he was dragged out of the room.

AT FIRST JACOB THOUGHT "HE" was the mayor of Middleburg. As it turned out, the true man pulling the strings was someone else. The actual mayor stood off to the side, nodding to a man wearing a black hood who was seated behind the mayor's desk. Light was supplied by candles on the desk.

Doctor Nguyen stood behind Jacob like a man at attention. "You are not needed, Doctor," the hooded man said.

"You injected my friend here with a sedative. I am concerned for his well-being. I prefer to remain and monitor him to make sure there are no serious after-effects," Nguyen said.

"Don't push your luck, Doctor," the hooded man said before turning his attention to Jacob. "Anyway, you said your name was Jacob Avery and that you're not from here. You came all this way just to rip off one of my pharmacies? You think I'm stupid?"

"I verified the evidence. He was sent here by a good friend of mine," Nguyen said.

"Let him speak for himself," barked the man in the hood.

"It's true." Jacob squirmed in his seat. "I didn't mean to steal your medicine, but I have to repay my doctor for helping my daughter. That's all. I'm desperate."

"And it didn't occur to you that we might need those supplies, seeing as how the lights are off for good? You think we're going to get a new shipment any time soon?"

"I know, I know," Jacob said. "I don't know what to tell you. Look, I care about your people too. I just didn't have any choice. What do you want me to do? I'll do anything if it lets me get back to my family with those supplies."

"Anything, huh?" the man in the hood asked. "Well, since you seem so willing, allow me to explain. I'm fortifying this town against the horrors to come. We're less than a thousand people. A small town means we can hold it together, but we need supplies to sustain us. Since you're willing to be a courier, perhaps you can put your services to work for us."

"You want me to get you something? What do you need? And where am I going?" Jacob asked.

"I'll give you the list. You won't go alone. You and a small team will head to Pleasantville."

"Wait, Pleasantville?" Jacob jumped out of his seat.

"It has what we need. You want to help? You will go. Then I'll allow you to leave with your goods."

Jacob's heart raced. Pleasantville, the very place he was trying to avoid?

"You ask a lot of him," said Nguyen sternly.

"It is my choice. He will do it or no medicine.

Even you must admit that it is a fair price," the hooded man said.

"For God's sakes." Nguyen strode up to the hooded man. "You are an efficient man, Trang, but compassion without efficiency is a mixture for brutality. Haven't I taught you better?"

The man under the hood scowled. "Hien..."

"And take off that hood. Jacob should know who you are...who we are."

The man at the desk discarded his hood, revealing a middle-aged man of Asian descent, with features much like Doctor Nguyen's. As the doctor turned, he smiled and pointed to the man beside him.

"Allow me to present Trang Nguyen, the current potentate of the town of Middleburg...and my younger brother."

FIND out what happens in part two!Available Now!

Made in the USA
Columbia, SC
19 December 2020

28843035R00140